SUMMER LION

LIZA FOSBURGH

SUMMER LION

William Morrow & Company
New York

Printed in the United States of America.
1 2 3 4 5 6 7 8 9 10

Library of Congress Cataloging-in-Publication Data
Fosburgh, Liza.
Summer lion.
Summary: Fourteen-year-old Leo's summer job with an
elderly man and his family in the Adirondacks gives him
self-confidence and a greater understanding of people.
1. Old age—Fiction. 2. Adirondack Mountains (N.Y.)—
Fiction. I. Title.
PZ7.F785Su 1987   [Fic]   87-12374
ISBN 0-688-06979-7

*In Fond Memory
of Leroy Whitney
and the Good Times*

SUMMER LION

The dirt road was long and dark beneath the trees, dipping in sharp curves down to the Boreas River, then climbing again. The sun burst through the leaves in spurts, only fully shining on the flat stretch over the one-lane bridge that spanned the river.

Leo sat tensely, one hand on the car window, the other clutching the seat. In all the years that he had lived less than two miles from this road, he had never been on it. That was a wonder in itself. He remembered his daddy talking about the good fishing on the Boreas and on Huntley Pond, but they had never come in together, to fish and spend the day. His daddy took him other places, to big lakes farther from home, where they got in the boat and spent hours going after the big ones on the bottom of the lake.

Now they approached Huntley Pond and the sun glistened on the flat surface, the rays dancing as a slight breeze crossed the water. It was much bigger than he had thought it would be.

"Not much farther now," his mother said. She looked at him and smiled. "I guess you're pretty excited. It's probably a little scary, too. First jobs usually are."

He nodded and stared at the road, once again darkened by shadows as they left Huntley and climbed the twisting, rocky road. Soon they passed a sign, "Beaver Mountain Club—Private Property—Members Only," and Leo knew there was no turning back now. He had wanted a summer job and he had been taken sight unseen by the Baines family. Of course, Mr. Baines knew his mother and had known his grandfather, so it wasn't as if Leo were a total stranger. Mr. Baines had arranged everything with Leo's mother, calling her way back in March from New York City to see if Leo was available. Leo had been recommended by Erastus Pike, who was the club superintendent. Leo didn't know Erastus real well, but his mother did and so did George. Come to think of it, Leo didn't know much of anybody or anything. He must have been living in some kind of shell all his life.

The club, which was primarily a fishing club for "very well-to-do people," as his mother had pointed out to him, spread across five thousand acres high in the Adirondack Mountains. It nestled at the base of Beaver Mountain, which rose almost three thousand feet into the air. The High Peaks—Marcy and McIntyre—rose even higher than that in the distance.

Leo gaped in wonder as the car banged and rattled over the loose dirt and rocks, past Mink Pond—too big to be called a pond, but tradition called it that—with its big slab-sided boat house, and on up the road to the sixty-acre clearing in the woods where members had their houses. He had no idea there could be so many big houses way back here in the woods. Tall trees stood singly or in groups of two or three, the rest having been cleared away to make room for this hidden community.

"It's this road to the right," his mother said, turning onto a rough, bumpy stretch that led to a big house. "They might all be out fishing. No, there's the Jeep. Somebody's probably home. I'm not going to spend much time here. I ought to get right back out. Do you mind?"

Leo panicked at the thought of her spending any time at all.

"I'll just run in and make sure they're here," she said.

"Don't do that," Leo quickly said. "I mean, I'd rather do it myself." He looked down at his hand holding on to the seat.

His mother stopped the car beside the Jeep, then reached over and patted his hand. "That's probably best. You're a big boy now and can handle things yourself."

He looked at her and nodded as she smiled at him. If she thought he just wanted to prove himself competent, that was all right with him.

"That's a nice big porch, with plenty of chairs," his mother said. "If they're not home, you've got a good place to wait."

Leo got out of the car and pulled his suitcase from the back seat. "You can go on now. I'll be all right."

"I'm sure you will be. You remember everything I told you and you'll do just fine. And if you need me, you go straight to the telephone. You'll remember, won't you?"

"Bye." He shut the car door and stepped back. He watched her back the car around at the very moment an old man appeared on the porch, limping toward the steps.

"Hold on there!" the old man called.

"Hello, Mr. Baines!" his mother shouted from the car window. "I've brought Leo!"

"Won't you come in?" Mr. Baines asked.

"I don't have time," she answered. "I've got to get back to work!"

"Don't worry about Leo! We'll take good care of him!"

"I'm sure you will," she called back. "Thank you!" She waved her hand and drove away.

Leo breathed a sigh of relief. That was one hurdle out of the way. He had been torn, wanting her to stay with him in this new situation and also not wanting her to get out of the car at all. The minute he saw the house, he knew which desire was the stronger.

"Come along, Leo," Mr. Baines said. "Time for us to get to know each other."

Leo shifted the suitcase from one hand to the other and headed for the steps.

"Do you like collard greens, Leo?" The old man looked down his long thin nose at the bamboo rod he was cleaning. His glasses sat about an inch down from where they should have been, and it was hard to tell if he was looking through them or over them.

"I don't think I've ever had them." Leo squirmed on the wooden slats of his porch chair, hoping no one would ask if he even knew what collard greens were. He was just guessing they were something to eat.

"Never had them?"

"No, sir."

"I think they're damned good myself. Of course, Miss Maudie . . ." Here he looked over the steel rims of the glasses at the old woman sitting across from him near the railing of the porch. "Miss Maudie won't have them in the house. Doesn't know what she's missing." He looked at Leo.

"No, sir." Leo squirmed again.

"I learned to like them when I was a boy, about your age . . . How old did you say you were?"

"He said he was fourteen," Miss Maudie answered sharply. "If you'd listen, you'd hear what people have to say."

"I did hear him, heard every word. I was just testing to see if you'd listened."

"Hmmmph!" Miss Maudie shifted in her chair so she was half turned away from him.

"As I was saying before I was interrupted, when I was about your age I spent a lot of time in the South bird-shooting. You do any bird-shooting around here, Leo?"

"No, sir." The first thing his mother had said to him when he got the job was "You be sure and say 'no, *sir*' and 'yes, *sir*' to Mr. Baines. He's a real gentleman and will expect no less."

"Bird-shooting's a fine sport," the old man continued in his gravelly quiet voice. "Of course, you've got to have a damned good dog, one that will work right with you, sniff out the bird, hold the point, all that. Many's the time we bagged fifty." Mr. Baines held the rod up to his eye and looked down the length of it. "I don't expect you have any objection to eating birds, do you?"

"No, sir." Leo had no idea what kind of birds he was talking about. He didn't figure anyone would take a "damned good dog" out to shoot fifty chickens.

"The boy doesn't even know what kind of birds you mean," Miss Maudie said, as if she were reading his mind. "You carry on as if everyone knew exactly what you meant." She leaned toward Leo. "He's talking about quail."

"I certainly am not. I'm talking about dove. Whoever heard of shooting fifty quail? You have no idea what you're saying. Try not to be influenced by Miss Maudie, Leo. She tends to get things mixed up."

"Hmmmph." She stuck her foot out and rubbed the sleeping brown-and-white dog with the toe of her oxford. The dog raised its head and began thumping its tail on the porch floor.

With that, two other dogs woke up, stood, stretched, and wandered over to the old woman's chair and began pushing their noses into her hands.

"Now what did you wake them up for?" Mr. Baines asked. "Don't you know about letting sleeping dogs lie?" He chuckled, a low gurgling sound deep in his throat. "That's another thing you're going to have to get used to," he said, grinning at Leo. "Miss Maudie and her dogs. You'll see."

Leo held his hand out to the white dog who wandered over to him. "Hi, doggie." He patted the dog's head. "What's his name?" he asked. He didn't know whether he was supposed to call Mr. Baines's sister "Miss Maudie" or "Miss Baines." He figured he'd better wait until she told him, though he knew most people called her "Miss Maudie." (Even his mother called her that: "And don't you forget to say *'ma'am'* to Miss Maudie when you answer her. She's a fine lady and will expect no less.")

"It's a she, and her name's Louisa."

Mr. Baines snorted. "Louisa. Hunting dogs ought to have short one-syllable names. Lou-is-a. It's too damned long, two syllables too long. Ought to call her 'Lou.'"

"Her name's Louisa," Miss Maudie repeated.

"You take a fine hunting dog like that and give her some damned-fool name and ruin her."

"She's not a hunting dog, are you, Louisa?" Miss Maudie clucked her tongue at the dog, who ran over to her chair and began pawing her.

"She should be a hunting dog. That dog's got some of the finest hunting blood in her veins that ever flowed in the South, and you bring her up here and make a lap dog out of her. Criminal. That's what it is: criminal. Don't you agree, Leo?"

Leo slid farther down in his chair and stared at the dog.

"And this is Nectarine," the old lady said, pointing to a medium-sized deep golden-orange dog with a short wiry-looking coat.

"Another fool name. Nectarine's a piece of fruit and has nothing to do with canines." Mr. Baines looked at Leo and winked. "I suppose if she'd been dark brown you'd have called her 'Fudge.'"

"Don't be ridiculous. Fudge would not be a proper name for a dog."

"That's totally irrational, isn't it, Leo? I remember when you were a little girl and you had a cat named Peppermint. Peppermint. And it wasn't red-and-white-striped either, was it? Logic isn't one of Miss Maudie's strong points. But I guess you'll find that out. Do you think Peppermint's a good name for a cat, Leo?"

"The boy's not going to answer a stupid question like that. And this one"—she continued to introduce the dogs to Leo—"this is Tossie."

"Don't even bother to ask where she got that name," Mr. Baines mumbled, blowing on the brass ferrules of the rod and polishing them with his handkerchief. "She probably can't remember anyway."

"I certainly can remember. The night she came we went to see *Tosca* and decided to name her that."

"You ever go to the opera, Leo?" Mr. Baines asked.

"No, sir." That was about as far away from his thinking as going to the moon.

"Good. It's a damned sight more expensive than a sleeping pill, and they both give you the same results."

"If you hadn't spent so much time hunting and fishing when you were young, you might have learned to appreciate music," Miss Maudie said.

"I expect I got more out of life being outdoors with good companionship than you did listening to a lot of screeching in foreign languages you can't even understand."

Miss Maudie stood up. "You never did have any

idea what you were saying on this subject. Don't listen to him, Leo. He just likes to ramble on."

Mr. Baines leaned back in his chair. "Leo. That's a fine name. Means 'lion,' but I expect you know that."

"Yes, sir."

"Leo the lion. Back when my grandchildren were growing up, we had baby-sitters for the summers and called them 'lion tamers.' Even before that, when my daughter was a little girl, we got lion tamers in to take care of the cousins and assorted friends that came to stay. I don't suppose they call them that anymore. Nowadays they probably call lion tamers something fancy like 'teaching companions.' " He chuckled, dipping his head down toward his chest, making his scrawny neck pull out of his shirt collar the way a turtle stretched its head out of its shell.

"What foolishness," Miss Maudie said, shaking her skinny leg to make her khaki pants leg go down.

"Is that so?" Mr. Baines looked up at her. "You tell me what they call them nowadays, if you know so much."

"They don't call them anything. People can't afford them now. People send their children to prenursery schools when they're little, and when they get older they send them to camp. People don't have help the way we had it. If you'd get your nose out of your tackle box, you might notice what's going on."

"Yes, I suppose you're right. People just don't have help the way we used to." Mr. Baines looked out across the meadow toward the mountains. Then suddenly he turned toward Leo and pointed a stiff gnarled finger at him. "Well, you're going to be my lion tamer, Leo, though a strapping youngster like you might really be the lion. But I like the idea of having a lion tamer. You don't mind being called that, do you?"

"No, sir." No one had ever called Leo "strapping." His mother said he was so skinny he didn't even cast a shadow.

"Don't take any guff from him, Leo. He'll give you a snow job any time he can," Miss Maudie said.

"Yes, ma'am." Leo had no idea what she was talking about, but she was staring at him so hard he had to answer something. "I don't mind."

"Don't mind what?" she asked.

Leo felt his neck turning red. "I mean, I don't mind being called that."

"Oh," she said. She pursed her lips and made a pinched smacking sound. The dogs began jumping up at her and dancing around her feet.

Leo smiled. "They sure act like they know what you're going to do."

"I guess they do," she answered. "Don't you, my pretties. Now you dogs go over there and get to know Leo. He's going to help take care of you this summer."

Mr. Baines grinned. "Bet you didn't know part of your job was going to be a dog-sitter. You ever handle dogs before?"

"No, sir. I mean, we've got an old dog at home, but

he mostly follows my mother around."

"You like dogs, don't you?" Miss Maudie asked.

"Oh, I sure do."

"Good. And I know they're going to like you. All you have to do is keep your eye on them sometimes. I feed them and all that."

"Yes, ma'am."

"We can't count on the grandchildren being too much help." When Miss Maudie said this, she gave her brother a real hard stare.

Mr. Baines smiled and nodded his head. "Miss Maudie gets upset because the young people like to sleep late."

"They waste the best part of the day."

"That's a matter of opinion," the old man answered. "Pookie and Tigger have different ideas."

"Hmmmph." Miss Maudie walked toward the door in little brisk steps. "It will be time for lunch in one hour."

"They'll be down by then. They always are."

"They better get started. They'll want a swim before lunch, I know. They always do." She held open the screen door. "Come on, dogs. Time to go wake up the sleepyheads."

The dogs raced past her into the house, bumping into her and sending her reeling against the doorjamb.

Leo held his breath. It wouldn't take much to knock her flat on the floor.

"Watch out!" she shouted, regaining her balance and following them into the house.

Mr. Baines chuckled again. "Miss Maudie and her dogs are a team. Your grandfather died, didn't he?"

"Yes, sir."

"That's too bad. Fine man. He was the road supervisor for many years, but I guess you know that."

"Yes, sir."

"Used to bring that big scraper all the way in here himself in the summer, about once a month. Did a fine job on the road. We never had any trouble with the road. When I first came here as a boy, we came in with a horse and buggy. The road was so bad, and we had those big long fancy cars we didn't dare bring over it. Used to leave them out at the hotel and come in with horses." He looked out, far away, again. "That was a long time ago. I had my eightieth birthday last year. Did you know that?"

"No, sir."

"Well, I did. Eighty years old. Eighty-one now. I've seen a lot. Not much has changed in here at the club, though. Lot of the same families are still here, and the new members are a fine bunch. We do have electricity and running water now. When I was a boy, we caught the rainwater on the roof and stored it right back up there"—he pointed to the top of the house—"up there at one end of the third floor in a big holding tank. Wonder the floor didn't cave in. But these cottages are so well made. No one's ever had any trouble. They don't make things like this anymore."

"No, sir." Leo's mother had told him they called these big houses "cottages," so his mouth didn't drop open when Mr. Baines said it. Sounded funny, though. A great big house that was even fancier than the hotel in town, all covered in log siding and called a "cottage." Rich people did queer things.

"This club has always been nice and simple. Not like some of the Adirondack clubs where you have to get dressed up in your penguin suit every night for dinner. No, sir, this place has always been run in a very simple fashion. It's for people who want to relax, get away, come here for some good fishing, enjoy the out-of-doors. That sort of thing. I expect you're quite the fisherman, coming from these parts."

Leo couldn't even get his mouth open. He didn't get to go fishing much anymore. His mother liked it, but she always went with George, and Leo usually stayed behind.

"It must be something to grow up surrounded by lakes," Mr. Baines went on. "When I used to sit behind a desk in the city, I'd dream about living up here year round. But then," he grinned at Leo, "if I hadn't been in the city, I wouldn't have been able to afford to come here."

"No, sir." He didn't know how much it cost to be a member of a club like this, but it must be a lot. Out in town it was just common knowledge that the members in here had plenty of money.

"You like to swim, too?" Without waiting for an answer, Mr. Baines continued, "My grandchildren are like fish in the water. Especially Pookie. Wait till you see her. Just like a seal. We spend a lot of time on the water. I don't swim much myself anymore, but we all like to fish. We picnic on the islands a lot, and of course, you have to row to them. Pookie sometimes swims over, but she's the only one. Pookie the seal. Slices through the water with barely a ripple."

Leo swallowed hard. "How many lakes are there?" he asked.

"Six. Three of them are trout-fishing only; two are for bass and pike; and one, Split Rock Pond, has bass and trout. Four of the lakes have fireplaces for cooking out and lean-tos for spending the night. The young people sleep out a lot. I'm too old now and like to come back to my own bed at night." He paused and studied the rod.

Leo waited, figuring there was more to come.

"There was a time, though, when I slept like a baby on those balsam needles. That's what happens when you get old: you miss out on a lot of simple pleasures, like sleeping under the stars and skinny-dipping at dawn." He chuckled in that low way again. "Miss Maudie thinks it's terrible the way the grandchildren cavort around, but she just forgets when we used to go skinny-dipping ourselves. Says she never did it. But I bet she did when the boys weren't looking." He peered over his glasses at Leo and grinned. "You look like a sensible, intelligent boy. I think we're going to get along just fine. Listen, I think I hear them coming."

The screen door banged open, and the three dogs rushed out, racing one another onto the deep porch that stretched around three sides of the house. As Leo watched them tumble about, playfully growling and snapping with their lips pulled over their teeth, the door opened again and a tall, blond, deeply tanned boy came out, squinting into the sunlight.

i, Grandpa."

"Tigger, my boy. Good to see you up. This is Leo, the boy who's come in to help me out this summer."

"Hi," Tigger said, raising a finger in acknowledgment.

"Hi." Leo leaned forward in his chair and looked at Tigger's cut-off blue jeans and gray T-shirt with a big red T on the back. He had no idea what that meant, and he didn't think any amount of guessing would give him the answer. "What's that T stand for?" he asked.

Tigger was facing the meadow, both hands on the railing to support himself. He turned his head and stared at Leo. "This shirt? M.I.T."

Leo said, "Oh," still not understanding what it meant. He felt his neck becoming red again.

"Tigger is a great rower," Mr. Baines said, coming to the rescue. "Crew has been his sport for some years now, and you should see the shirts he's collected."

Leo must have looked really stupid, because Mr. Baines explained further, "In rowing—that's crew— the boat that wins the race also wins the shirts from the other rowers who didn't win. That's where the term 'betting your shirt' came from. I expect you know that saying."

Leo had never heard of it, but he nodded.

"Tigger's boat is so good, he walks off with an armload of shirts every season. And he's been doing it for seven years, so you can imagine the number of shirts he has."

"You in college?" Leo asked Tigger.

Tigger nodded. "Princeton."

Well, Leo had heard of Princeton all right. He knew it was about the best university there was, that and Yale and some others. Boy, Tigger sure must be smart. "I'll be in ninth grade," he said.

Tigger nodded his head in response.

"Where's your sister?" Mr. Baines asked.

"She's coming." Tigger looked toward the door.

"You going to try to get in some breakfast?" Mr. Baines asked.

"Not if Miss Maudie's got lunch scheduled for twelve-thirty."

"I expect you'll go for a swim."

"Soon as Pookie gets here. Why don't you come, too, Grandpa?"

"No, thank you, Tigger, my boy. Not today. Leo and I are just going to take it easy on the porch this morning. Now, Leo . . ." the old man turned to face Leo, "I take a nap in the afternoons, and during that time you can do whatever you want. Swim. Hike. Even sleep. I don't get going again until about three."

"Four, Grandpa, four. It takes you an hour to wake up."

Mr. Baines tucked his head down onto his throat and laughed a low gurgling laugh. "They keep a pretty close watch on me, Leo. Pretty close."

"Hi, Grandpa," a small, quiet voice said.

Leo jumped. He hadn't even heard the door open.

"There you are, Pookie, darling. Come give Grandpa a kiss."

Leo watched as a slight apparition of a girl about halfway between his and Tigger's age moved gingerly across the floor, as if it were covered in eggs. She bent and kissed her grandfather's cheek, then slid slowly to the railing to stand next to Tigger.

"This is Leo," Mr. Baines said. Then to Leo, "I don't think Pookie's quite awake."

Pookie turned her head and smiled gently at her grandfather.

"You don't look like you're dressed for swimming," Mr. Baines said to her.

Leo thought she looked as if she was dressed for a sideshow. Her feet were stuck into dirty sneakers with plenty of holes and no shoelaces. Above that she had on white winter-underwear bottoms, and they had shrunk something terrible because they only came about halfway down her calf. Over that, she wore a white loose man's shirt that came almost to her knees and looked as if she'd slept in it, it was that wrinkled. Her hair, which was real short in one of those punk cuts, stood up in straggly tufts like a month-old crew cut.

"You'd better get on down to the lake," Mr. Baines said, tapping Tigger on the back with the tip of his rod. "I expect Miss Maudie'll have something good for lunch. She usually does," he added to Leo. "When I was a boy, we never ate in the cottages. Everyone ate up at the dining room. Now things have changed. I still have breakfast up there, but everyone else has it here. We have lunch here so the young people can be more flexible in their hours. Then we all eat dinner in the dining room. Except when we picnic."

"You ready?" Tigger asked his sister.

Pookie nodded, a slow sleepy nod in which she barely moved her head. She turned around, with one hand still on the railing, and looked at Leo.

"This rod got awful dried out over the winter," Mr. Baines said. "But I think this oil will help it. Not my favorite one anyway. Still, there's no point in not taking care of it."

Pookie turned to Tigger and whispered, "Who's that?"

Tigger looked at Leo. "That's Leo. You know, the one who's come in to help Grandpa."

"Oh, hi," she said, smiling and taking a step toward Leo with her hand outstretched.

Leo was so far back in his chair, he had to use his hands to pull himself out. He made it and stuck out his hand. "Hi." Her hand felt like a flat little piece of silk that had never had a bone in it.

She stood staring at him, smiling in a friendly way, and he thought she must be looking at his clothes.

Leo shifted from one foot to the other and sat back down. He knew his pants looked funny. They were way too big, but his mother had made him wear them anyway. "Just pull them up and tighten your belt," she'd said. "They're good pants, L. L. Bean, and I'm not about to throw them out because you'd rather wear your old blue jeans. Those people in at the club all wear khaki pants and look nice, and you just be thankful your cousin Bert outgrew them and gave them to you." It was a sure bet his mother had never seen anyone wearing long underwear right out in the open in the summertime. Leo felt his face going red again, wishing he hadn't listened to her.

"Let's go," Tigger said, giving Pookie a push with the palm of his hand in the middle of her back.

"Will you come with us?" Pookie asked Leo. "It's real nice down at Mink. It's where everyone goes to swim."

Leo shook his head.

"Maybe next time," she said.

Tigger prodded her again and finally took her arm and led her away.

Leo wondered if Tigger had to steer Pookie around a lot. She didn't seem too motivated.

After Leo and Mr. Baines were alone on the porch, they heard the sound of a rough motor revving up, then the crunching of gravel.

"The walk down to Mink's not so bad," Mr. Baines said, "but that hill is a killer coming back up. They always use the Jeep. Sometimes Tigger thinks he owns the damned thing. I'm pretty lenient with him about using it, as long as it doesn't interfere with my needing it. You old enough to drive?"

"No, sir." His mother had wanted to teach him this past spring, but George had said, "No way. He's not going to get a chance to total my car for another year." And that ended that. Leo looked down at his khaki pants. When he could get up to his room, he'd put on his old blue jeans that he had packed when his mother wasn't looking, the faded ones with the hole in the knee and the ripped pocket. His mother sure was square sometimes.

"Now, Leo," Mr. Baines said quietly, looking toward the screen door. "I like to have a little toddy before lunch. Helps me to sleep in the afternoons. I don't think Miss Maudie likes for me to drink anything; she probably thinks it's bad for my blood pressure. She's never actually said so, but I can tell, and I don't want to upset her. I'll tell you something, though—she doesn't know what's right all the time. Good heart, but in the wrong place sometimes. Now here's what I want you to do."

And Leo got started right off being a conspirator for Mr. Baines's drinking secrets. He didn't mind. He'd been around drunks and lesser drinkers all his life, what with his mother being a waitress at the hotel and Leo spending every school-day evening in a corner of the bar doing his homework while his mother took a shift being bartender if she wasn't still waiting tables. No, he didn't mind sneaking into the linen closet and finding Mr. Baines's hidden bottle and putting a splash into his iced tea. It was all part of his summer job to him.

"Hey, Highpockets," a small voice said behind him as Leo stood at the porch railing watching three deer graze in the meadow. He felt his face getting hot and figured it must be about ten shades of red. He turned as little as possible to look at Pookie.

She moved slowly to stand beside him, glancing down at his khaki pants as she negotiated her feet into a balancing position.

Leo didn't know why he was standing there when he could have been upstairs getting his blue jeans, but Miss Maudie had sent him outside to shoo away a rabbit that she said was going to send the dogs on a chase, and he'd only gotten back this far when he noticed the deer.

"You'll have to eat a lot of Miss Maudie's muffins to fill out those pants." Pookie squinted into the light.

Leo wished she'd just shut up about them.

"Don't worry about it," she went on, her voice slipping into a tiny sound. "By the end of summer you'll have trouble getting into any of your clothes. Grandpa calls Miss Maudie a feeder. I guess she is."

Leo managed to find his voice. "You don't look like you eat much."

Pookie just stared into the light.

"See those deer?" Leo asked her, trying to think of something to talk about.

"Where?"

"Over there, by that big tall fir tree."

"Oh, yes. There are lots of deer."

Leo could tell he wasn't going to get far with that subject. He finished up, "We don't see many out in town. Guess they're all in here." He waited a second or so, then said, "Well, guess I'll go on in."

"Oh, I was supposed to tell you . . ." Pookie turned her head and leaned it toward Leo.

He waited.

"Oh, yes, it's about dinner," she whispered to him.

Leo looked behind him to see if anyone was listening. That big long porch was as empty as a tunnel after the train had gone through. "What is it?" he whispered back, unable to help himself.

"It's about dinner," she repeated.

Leo leaned toward her in order to hear her.

"Miss Maudie says we're not going to eat at the dining room tonight—you know, the one by the clubhouse—but are going to picnic at Mink Island instead." She whispered it so quietly it was like a little breeze rustling the leaves at the very top of the trees. She frowned and stared at him, apparently trying to tell if he'd understood her.

Leo nodded. He couldn't think of anything to say.

Pookie reached down and touched the hem of her shirt as if she were trying to figure out what it was. "I hope you like to picnic. Some people are bothered by the black flies this time of year. Are you allergic to them?"

"No, they don't bother me a bit."

"Me neither," she said. "No one in our family is allergic to them. We're glad you've come. Grandpa needs someone strong to be with him, and Tigger and I will like having someone our age around. Do you play cards?"

"A little."

"Three people can play Finnish Eights, and there's always Yahtzee. I have to go get ready for lunch." She slid one foot in front of the other and silently went away.

Leo got a warm feeling watching her. She was pretty vague, but she was nice. She treated him like . . . well, like one of the club members, not like some dumb jerk from town. Yeah, she was all right.

Picnic. That meant going on the water. He'd better tell Mr. Baines what a good rower he was. With luck, that would be all he'd be expected to do.

Someone should have taught him how to swim long before now. His mother had time on her days off. And George was a good swimmer, but he sure wouldn't do anything to help Leo. He was only interested in Leo's mother. George could do a lot of things. He could swim and drive any kind of car or tractor, and he could fish and shoot—all kinds of things. He could run that hotel with one hand tied behind his back. Leo's mother said that all the time. "George can order the stock and keep books and bartend and mend anything that needs repairing, from the crack of dawn to a broken heart, and all that with one hand tied behind his back." That was a favorite saying of George's: "I can mend anything, from the crack of dawn to a broken heart." He'd say that when the bar got filled up, and then they'd all laugh, George the loudest just as if he was saying it for the first time. Yes, sir, George could do anything, anything but teach Leo how to do things.

Leo peeled a piece of bark from the log railing. Well, this was his chance to teach himself how to swim. He didn't need George. Or his mother. If he had to learn,

26

he would. If he wanted to learn, he could. Then he could go swimming with Tigger and Pookie before lunch and could play cards with them later, after dinner. He could get to be real friends with them.

Tigger and Pookie. They had funny names, but they seemed okay.

ou're not eating much, Leo," Miss Maudie said, passing him the butter dish. "You're not coming down with that bug that's going around, are you? I expect it's out in town the same as it's in here."

"No, ma'am."

They were all sitting around the kitchen table having lunch. It was a real big kitchen, with dark paneled walls and ceiling, a big black stove with fancy ironwork on it on one side of the room, and a modern gas range and refrigerator on the other side. In between, one wall held an old-fashioned sink that stood on spindly iron legs next to a dishwasher. Rows and rows of shelves filled with china, canned goods, and cartons took up the fourth wall.

"What bug is that?" Mr. Baines asked, peering over the rims of his glasses as he buttered a muffin.

"The one young Tommy van Allston's got."

Mr. Baines stopped buttering and looked at his sister. "Maybe he's finally developed an allergy to all those plastic worms he uses."

"What nonsense," Miss Maudie retorted. "He's got a bug. Stomach bug. Mrs. McAllister told me when I looked in on her this morning."

"How is her tooth?" Mr. Baines asked.

"Not much better. Rastus is going to drive her out to the dentist this afternoon."

"Anybody else got that bug?" Mr. Baines asked, resuming his buttering.

"Not yet, unless Leo has it."

"No, ma'am. I feel fine." The newness of everything had made him feel a little strange, but he wasn't going to say that.

"Perhaps you'd like to ask your mother in for dinner tomorrow," Miss Maudie said.

Leo felt his stomach lurch. "She has to work tomorrow night," he said quickly.

"Well, maybe you'd like to have her come in and picnic with us tonight," she continued, not dropping the subject the way Leo wished she would, but going on like a dog with a bone.

"Say," Mr. Baines chimed in, "that's a good idea. Why don't you call her and see if she can come back in, Leo?"

Leo felt his neck going red. He picked up his muffin. "She can't do that. It's not her night off. And when she does get one, she usually keeps busy." He shoved the muffin into his mouth.

Tigger leaned back in his chair. "Summers are good times to get away from mothers. Pass me the milk, Pookie." He paused. "Pookie?"

She raised her head and smiled at him.

"Milk," Tigger repeated.

"Oh, sure." She picked up the carton with both hands and leaned toward Tigger.

Leo stopped chewing and watched her. She was acting queer. He hoped she wouldn't lean any farther—another inch and she might keep going and land on the floor. Tigger got the carton, and Pookie slowly reeled back to an upright position.

"Try to eat some of that omelet, Pookie," Miss Maudie said. "It's one of your favorites."

"Oh, I know." Pookie slowly turned her head toward Miss Maudie. "I like it. I really do."

"Good. Then eat some more of it."

Leo looked at his plate, not wanting to stare at Pookie. He had managed to eat half of his omelet, but he still had a lot of creamed potatoes left and he hadn't touched the salad yet. Another day and he would have had three or four muffins by now, but he was just finishing his first one. He got some potatoes on his fork and into his mouth.

Pookie's mouth was open a little, as if she were having a hard time breathing through her nose. She was staring just beyond her plate, at some invisible spot on the top edge of her place mat. Her shoulders had drooped, and now her head had sunk an inch more toward her chest. She reminded Leo of a child being punished in front of the class, sitting alone in another world with just a lot of terrible thoughts.

He looked down at his own plate. A few more bites would make a dent in the potatoes. Then he'd tackle some of the salad, if his stomach held up. He felt ashamed of himself for not wanting his mother to come in. It was just the sort of thing she'd like to do: come in here with a lot of shiny tackle and a flashy spinning rod and have a wonderful time going around the lakes catching a lot of fish. And she wouldn't care one hoot about the way she looked. She had never cared much about public opinion. Once, when Leo was real small, he had wet his pants when he was walking down the street with her, and she had just taken his hand and said, "Never mind. Let them stare if they want to. If God hadn't wanted you to do that, you wouldn't have done it. So there." Even though he had been small, he still remembered it. And he remembered how she'd hugged him as soon as they got in the car.

Pookie slipped a notch forward and knocked her fork off her plate. This made her hunch up her shoulders and draw back. She looked so small, sitting there all screwed up; her eyes had contracted and her forehead bunched in a frown. Leo was afraid that she had some kind of food poisoning, but no one else seemed to notice.

"I'll take part of your omelet," Tigger said to her.

She nodded gratefully at him and watched as he slid half her food off her plate onto his own.

Miss Maudie clucked her tongue softly and pushed back her chair. "I sliced some peaches for dessert. Maybe those will go down easier."

While she didn't name anyone specifically, Leo figured everyone knew she was talking to Pookie. He watched her open the refrigerator door and bring out a big bowl covered in plastic wrap.

"The peaches we got when we were young were something out of this world," Mr. Baines said. "Big, plump things that dribbled juice down your chin when you bit them. Remember? Remember how big they were? I don't know how they managed to grow them without pesticides and fertilizers and the usual variety of chemicals they use now."

"They had fewer trees in an orchard and could give them special attention, for one thing, and then they used plenty of cow manure," Miss Maudie answered.

"Is that so?" He looked across the room at his sister. "Think they just turned the cows loose in the orchards?"

"No, I think they cleaned out their barns and put it to good use."

"Remember how good the peaches tasted?"

"They were good then and they're good now." Miss Maudie looked at Pookie's plate.

Tigger waited for Miss Maudie to nod at him; then he quietly took the rest of Pookie's food, this time just eating it right off her plate, which he wedged in beside his own.

"When we were children, we never would have done a thing like that," Mr. Baines said, peering at Tigger. "Mother would have been scandalized if we had taken food from someone's plate. Anything that was left over on your plate went to the trash."

"No," Miss Maudie said, "it went to the kitchen. You have no idea what happened to it after that."

Mr. Baines let the muffin drop from his crooked fingers, and his shoulders shook up and down as he chuckled. "You're absolutely right. It may well have been eaten by someone. Maybe the dogs got it. I don't know how I'd remember anything accurately if I didn't have Miss Maudie to keep a tight rein on me." He got a grip on his muffin and took a bite. "I don't suppose it matters if you eat off someone's plate, as long as it's someone you know. And I'm sure you don't have any germs, do you, Pookie, darling."

Miss Maudie placed a small dish of sliced peaches in front of Pookie. "Try these. They're those good New York State peaches. Here's a little cream for them. Grandpa might not like them as much as the ones in his recollections, but you don't have that complication. And the cream is not straight out of the cow in the barn. It's via a lot of sanitary machinery and a paper carton, but it tastes all right."

Pookie looked up at her and smiled. She poured cream on the peaches and put a slice in her mouth. After she had chewed it and swallowed, she turned to Miss Maudie. "Thank you," she whispered. Then she put down her spoon and let her head droop.

Mr. Baines drove the Jeep as if it were a tank. His bony gnarled hands gripped the wheel tightly as they rumbled forward in low gear, not bothering to dodge rocks sticking up in the middle of the road, but just rolling over them with a lurch and a crash that made Leo gasp and clutch the door frame.

"These damned rocks," Mr. Baines would mutter, his eyes straight ahead. He sat leaning back on the seat, his arms out straight, his neck craning forward from his collar. "Don't let that rod bounce up and down" was a frequent command to Leo. That and "Look over there!" Leo never knew what he was supposed to be looking at. Between holding on to the rod and watching the rocks coming up at them, he never saw anything "over there" or anywhere else, except the big houses slipping by.

Mr. Baines had decided to give Leo a tour of the clearing before they drove down to Mink Pond. With its unpaved roads, it was more like a little village than he had at first realized, only there weren't any stores or anything like that. Just those "cottages" and the clubhouse, which was a big log-sided building encircled by deep porches and hooked by a covered walkway to another building that Mr. Baines said was the dining room and kitchen. "The cook and the kitchen help live in rooms over the kitchen," he explained as they shuddered slowly past, the Jeep almost but not quite choking to a halt, as Mr. Baines depressed the accelerator and they groaned forward again. "Damned fine cook, too. You'll like eating dinners over there. She makes a pie like you never tasted. Your mother a good cook? Don't let that rod bounce up and down."

"Yes, sir." When she bothered to cook. Mostly they ate at the hotel. That was all right now. The new hotel cook was better than the last one, who burned so much George said charcoal must be her favorite taste. It was when she was there that Leo gave up eating eggs.

As they rumbled past the houses, all kinds of people would call out to them from their porches, waving and being real friendly like, but Mr. Baines never looked to the right or left, just stared through those steel-rimmed glasses that sat down on his nose like permanent fixtures. However, he seemed to know who they were without looking.

"That's old Mrs. Pearson, probably as old as I am, and gets around at about the same speed." Or: "Young

Tommy van Allston over there never has learned how to fly-fish. He just drops sinkers and plastic worms and those Christmas-tree hooks over the side of the boat and brings in a big bass and calls it fishing. He's twenty years old and ought to know better. Look over there!" And: "That's probably Beek asleep in that hammock on her grandmother's porch. You know Beek? No, probably not. She's a friend of Tigger's. Pookie's, too. Great girl. I'd just like to plan on Tigger marrying her some day. Watch the rod."

Mr. Baines took a corner at crawl speed, the front right wheel going up so high on a big rock that Leo thought for sure they would flip over. But they just ground on, bucking and chewing up the road a little before they smoothed out.

"Now here comes Creeper McGraw. He's the club president. Damned fine one, too. He's been coming here since he was in diapers." Mr. Baines chuckled. "He was in them long enough, too. That's how he got his name: he crawled on all fours, bundled up in baby clothes, so long he almost wore out his knees. However, once he stood up he rose right to the top. Top of everything: school, college, the brokerage firm. He's been president of the club for two years. I'd like to see him stay in another ten."

Leo clutched the rod, wishing his mother had taught him how to drive a car. Then he could be driving the old man around right now. It was bound to hurt his arthritic hands holding on to the wheel like that. Leo bet Tigger had been taught to drive by the time he was fourteen. These rich people had so much money, it wouldn't matter to them if a car got a little dent on it by someone learning how to drive. They'd just have it fixed out at Sporty's Body Shop and that would be that.

"We'd better get on down to the lake. Miss Maudie and the dogs walk pretty fast, and we don't want to keep her waiting. If I know Tigger, he'll be out in his canoe trying to get one of those big browns. He's a fine fisherman. Taught him myself, back when I could get around better. We'd get up early and go to a lake long before anyone else was awake. He could cast like a pro by the time he was ten. My daughter—that's his mother—she's pretty good, too. Pretty good. It's in their blood. Now Pookie, she could be good, but she gets distracted. She never did have enough attention span, and you can't learn to fish without that. Did you notice if she went to the lake when Tigger went?"

"No, sir."

"Tigger's pretty good about rounding her up, so I guess she did. I guess he took the station wagon. You think your mother would mind if you learned how to drive?"

"No, sir!"

"Good. I can manage driving around the clearing and down to Mink, but it's a devil of a job for me to try to get this thing over to Frank Pond or Split Rock. Tigger just drops everything and drives me over when he knows I want to go, but there are times I feel bad about dragging him away from a game of tennis or something around here with the other young people. But you could handle this all right." He chuckled again. "It's like fighting a bucking mule, taking this Jeep over those rough log roads. Used to be a damned sight easier when we had to walk every place. Now no one walks, except the old-timers who can still manage to get around. The new generation is soft. Pretty soft. Don't let that rod bounce up and down. But they've got other qualities, and that makes up for their lack of stamina. People just have too much now. Excess isn't necessarily bad, but it's not good either. Don't you agree?"

"Yes, sir." He'd never had too much of anything in his life, except that time Peaches Cranshaw bet him he couldn't eat the rest of the pancakes left over from the church pancake supper, and he ate them and oh, boy ... winning that five dollars sure wasn't worth the stomachache he had for two days. His mother was hopping mad at him, but she still kept coming into his room to see how he felt and brought him weak tea, which he didn't drink, but he liked her trying to be nice to him after he'd been a jerk. George chomped down on a cigar in the corner of his mouth and said, "Serves him right," and after Leo got over the ordeal and went into the bar to do his homework, George made snide references to the "pancake-eater," and even went so far as to say, "I thought I could fix anything, from the crack of dawn to a broken heart, but a fool with ten pounds of pancakes in him just buffaloed me. Said he ought to call the vet who was used to irrigating cows." Everybody laughed.

Leo tried to look at the old man, but his eyes kept going back to the road. "Sure are a lot of rocks."

"You just have to learn how to avoid them," Mr. Baines said.

"Yes, sir."

"A little practice and you'll get the hang of it."

"Yes, sir."

"We'll start tomorrow morning. That all right with you?"

"Yes, sir. It sure is."

"Good. Look over there! There's a big population this summer. Must not be as many foxes about."

"What is it?"

"Hares! Use your eyes. You've got to be observant."

"Hairs?" He automatically reached up and touched his head.

"Sure. Hares. Big rabbits. Not the little cottontails you get out on farms, but the 'varying hares' that turn white in the winter. Masters of camouflage. You probably call them snowshoe rabbits."

Leo wasn't sure he'd ever called them anything. He

wasn't even sure he'd ever thought about them. "Oh. Yes, sir. I missed it."

"Pookie never sees anything. She never learned to be observant. My father used to take us on a walk, and at the end of it we had to write down everything we'd seen. The one with the biggest list got a reward. I had two brothers, and my sister Maudie and each of the four of us tried real hard to see more than the other three." He bobbed his head up and down in silent laughter. "We were pretty good. It made us observant, I'll tell you that. My brothers were younger than we were and they're both dead. What do you think of that? Tell you what: I might row Miss Maudie and Pookie over to the island and let you come in another boat with the dogs."

"That's fine." Leo breathed a sigh of relief.

"We'll have to take two boats, with four people, three dogs, and the picnic food. And just between you and me, Leo, I'd just as soon not go in the boat with the dogs. But you're young and you won't have any trouble. It's just hard on my rowing having them wandering all over the boat. Not as strong as I used to be. You're sure that's all right with you?"

"Yes, sir." Leo had known how to row a boat for a long time. His daddy had taught him that, way back, when they used to go out fishing for bass and pike and his daddy would sit in the back of the rowboat and say "Move us along here real slow, Leo. Those big lunkers are hiding just at the edge of those weeds, and we're going to trail this silver minnow just under their noses and get ready for them to smash it." And he'd give a big smile and reach his big hand up and steady the oars, sometimes giving them a little push so they moved along at just the right speed. Leo could have done it all himself, even though he was pretty little at the time. But he never minded his daddy helping. "I like to row," he said.

"Now don't let the rod bounce up and down. We're about to go down this hill and it's pretty rough. Pretty rough."

And the Jeep picked up speed and kicked up gravel and sand as it roared down the hill, just as if it had a mind of its own and was in a hurry to get to Mink Pond and take a much-needed rest under the balsams by the water's edge.

Now, Leo," Miss Maudie said, grabbing a picnic basket and swinging it into the wide, round-bottomed guide boat, "you just get the dogs in that green rowboat and let us take the rest of the things. Get over here, Louisa! You'd better hurry and get in, or she'll get on a bird's trail and disappear on you. You ready?" she asked Mr. Baines.

"Just waiting for you." Mr. Baines sat in the middle of the guide boat, which Leo thought looked like a double-ended, oversized wooden canoe.

"Where's Pookie?" Miss Maudie asked, looking around.

"I think she's out in the canoe with Tigger." Mr. Baines squinted across the lake.

Miss Maudie put her hand above her eyes to shade them from the late afternoon sun and peered in the direction her brother indicated. "Oh, yes. There she is. Well, I've got everything in."

"Except yourself." Mr. Baines held the boat steady with one hand on the dock. "Hurry up. We don't want to sit here all night."

"Get the dogs, Leo!" Miss Maudie called as she sat down on the dock and swung her skinny legs into the boat. Once settled in her stern seat facing Mr. Baines, she snapped, "Well, let's go!"

Leo called, "Tossie! Nectarine! Louisa!" Miss Maudie had drilled him on the dogs' names as soon as he got out of the Jeep, and she must have done a pretty good job. He whistled as loudly as he could. "Tossie! Oh, good, here you are. Hop in."

The brown-and-white dog hopped in the rowboat and sat on the seat watching the guide boat ease out of the dock slip.

"Good girl. You just stay there. Nectarine! Louisa!" He wished they'd hurry and come. If he had to stand there in the boat shouting for them he was going to look like a fool and get Miss Maudie mad at him for being an incompetent. "Louisa!" He could see a white flash through the trees, heading back toward the boat house. "Oh, good," he mumbled under his breath. "Nectarine!"

Louisa raced onto the dock and threw herself into the boat, nearly knocking Leo down. He lurched forward and grabbed the side of the dock. "Oh, wow. That's all I need." He figured he'd better step out of the boat and wait on the dock for Nectarine to show up or he'd be a goner for sure, right into that dark Adirondack water.

"Nectarine!" He held the painter rope tied to the bow of the boat securely in his hand and stepped back toward the boathouse entrance.

That was a mistake. Louisa and Tossie both hopped out of the boat and followed him.

"No, no. You get back in there. Louisa! Come back here!" He watched as the white dog raced out onto the path and headed for the woods. "Louisa!"

Louisa abruptly turned and raced back toward him.

"Here. Get in the boat." Leo went back to the side and pointed into the boat.

Louisa jumped in, knocking one oar that rattled and clattered across the wooden seat like a machine-gun burst.

Leo winced and looked out at the guide boat. Both the old people had turned to look at him.

"Now sit down," he said in a hushed voice. "Here. You, Tossie. Get back in." Tossie obeyed, and Leo felt his heart begin to race. How was he going to keep them there while he went to look for Nectarine?

"Nectarine!"

He'd barely gotten the word out before the wiry golden-orange dog appeared, dripping wet, with a long lily-pad stem draped across her back.

"Here. Get in here. Get in." Leo gave the wet rear end a push, and Nectarine dropped down into the boat, standing just between the oar locks. "Move over." Leo tried to push her out of the way as he hurriedly climbed into the boat. He was so afraid one of them would escape before he got away from the dock that he forget to put the painter into the boat, simply dropping it into the water. He pushed the boat along the dock with his hands and gave it a final shove past the escape routes and out into the open water. Then he looked back at the rope trailing in the water. "Oh, no." He'd have to climb back there and pull it in. If Mr. Baines saw it like that, he'd think Leo didn't know anything. He turned and started to stand up, but as he did, the three dogs began to run from side to side, rocking the boat almost out of control. "Sit down!" He quickly dropped to the seat.

Nectarine returned to stand right in front of Leo, right where his legs ought to be and right where the oars *had* to be.

"Move." He pushed her away with his foot, hoping Miss Maudie wouldn't turn around at that very moment.

Nectarine obligingly went to the stern to sit beside Tossie, who was taking on a bored, sleepy look. Louisa stood in the bow, shifting from foot to foot and side to side, but at least not jumping out.

Leo began to row. This was some fine lake. It was better than any he'd ever been on, because there were no houses to be seen around the shore, just wilderness.

He glanced back at the boathouse. It looked real impressive from the water, with its long peaked roof and the four boat slips, each one wide enough for two boats across and long enough for two deep. At either side of the boat house were deep decks, with ladders for swimmers and chairs for watchers. About fifty feet out was a big raft, also with a ladder. This must be where Pookie and Tigger swam before lunch.

Far to the left of the boathouse, near the shore, a big rock that Mr. Baines had called Sunfish Rock protruded from the water. To the right of the boathouse was a stretch of thick water lilies and just beyond it another dock. Up the bank were a bunch of canoes resting upside down, and beyond them a small building with more canoes resting on rafter-like structures. Leo stared at them in wonder. Just about everyone here must have a canoe, maybe more than one.

Nowhere was there a sign of a motor boat or an outboard motor. Leo guessed that was the way things were in here: silence on the lakes. His daddy had had a fine outboard motor on the back of his big metal bass boat. He was real proud of it. Treated it like a Cadillac.

Suddenly Nectarine's ears went up and her body tensed. She jumped from the seat and mashed her body against the side of the boat. Leo's stomach turned right over as he spotted the loon cruising through the water, right toward them.

The bird's jet-black head turned gracefully from side to side, then back again, held erect above the V-shaped ripples fanning out in its wake. Its body was low on the surface, barely noticeable from a distance. Suddenly its head went under and it disappeared in a silent dive.

Nectarine ran to the other side of the boat, throwing Leo off balance and making one of his oars come out of the water with a great splash.

"Sit down! Sit!" He tried to say it as fiercely and as quietly as he could. "Sit down!" He nervously looked ahead at the guide boat, hoping they hadn't seen his oar slapping at the water. It made a terrible noise in all this silence. He slowed his stroke.

Nectarine ran up and tried to get past him to the front of the boat.

"Go on back! Back!" He hissed. He gave her body a push with one oar as he brought them both forward and tried to drop them into the water for a continuing stroke. But Nectarine stood firmly in his way. "Back!" He had to stop rowing altogether, hold both of the oar grips in one hand as he used the other hand to push the dog. "Back!" She was as solid as a rock. It was like trying to push a bull.

The loon emerged, nearer to the rowboat. It raised its beak skyward, and the high clear laughing sound echoed sharply and loudly across the lake.

Nectarine forgot about her intention to get past Leo

and ran back and hung over the side of the boat, panting and trembling.

Louisa started to bark and run around in the front of the boat, almost pushing Leo off his seat in her excitement. She whammed into his back each time she ran from side to side.

Tossie perked up her ears in interest, and retained her dignity by sitting quietly.

It was impossible to row, with the running around and the barking, to say nothing of the hysterical panting and trembling. "Sit! Sit down! No! No!" Leo forgot to lower his voice, and it now sounded as if he were shouting at someone on the far shore.

In all this disturbance, the loon dived under the water. The two troublesome dogs suddenly stopped and threw themselves against the side of the boat to stare at the widening circles of water left by the submerged loon.

Leo's hands were shaking. He thought the boat was going to turn over for sure; then what would he do? He probably wouldn't even be able to save himself, let alone try to rescue the dogs. He looked at the guide boat and saw that he was being watched. He then turned his head toward the direction of the red canoe. It, too, rested still in the water, and the two heads were turned in his direction.

He shifted over a few inches on his seat to counterbalance the weight of the two dogs hanging over the side. Boy, it was hard to row with them like that. He concentrated real hard, trying to keep the oars level so they wouldn't splash water like some paddle wheel.

The late-afternoon sun slanted across the water to the trees on the eastern shore. He felt a familiar twinge of loneliness, the one that had begun two years before after his daddy was killed in that smashup on the highway. The late afternoon, when his daddy had come home from work, had been the worst time of the day to face. There was no one to talk to, nothing to do except sit by himself and wait, feeling the void in the house as strongly as something he could touch.

When his daddy had been alive, his mother went over to the hotel at mealtimes to wait tables and sometimes to help out in the kitchen if they had a crowd coming. Leo was always home in the afternoons, doing his homework or watching television or playing with some of the boys from school. Then, when his daddy came, they'd throw the football around until it was time to eat or do something special like going down the highway to bring back pizzas for dinner. If it was a slow night at the hotel, his mother would be there with them. But not after his daddy died. Then she spent her spare time with George.

He was sure his mother had been lonely, the same as he had been, but she had her work. She had people all around her, and even if they were strangers, they talked and laughed and reached out when she needed them. And she had George, who was right there as soon as it happened, of course. Besides being at the hotel, he was always in and out of the house. Soon—way too soon to suit Leo—he just moved in with them and established himself as the new head of the household.

And once George took over, Leo and his mother spent nearly all their time at the hotel, just coming home to go to bed. Leo understood that as the manager George had to be there, but he sure didn't like it. He felt about as uncomfortable and conspicuous as that old stuffed coyote head over the bar. There wasn't a corner dark enough for him to hide in; everyone who came in saw him and stared.

He got out of the habit of doing things with the other boys after school. They didn't like coming to the hotel and playing in the parking lot, and Leo sure didn't blame them for that. And his mother got nervous when he said he was going to get a ride over to so-and-so's house for a while. It seemed as though she wanted him in her sight all the time.

The canoe slid beside the narrow wooden dock at the island. It was a real pretty red and stood out against the dark greens and blacks of the woods and water. He could see Pookie disappearing into the trees, while Tigger waited on the dock, ready to help the old people out of the guide boat. Leo pulled on the oars, really putting his back into it.

George never hit Leo or anything like that. But he

sure could chew him out when he put his mind to it. Like the time Leo decided to build a fire in that little fireplace they never used. Hell's bells, it was a fireplace—how was he to know the chimney would catch fire? George not only yelled at him about it, he had a real shouting session with Leo's mother. That was before George had moved in with them and Leo had been allowed to spend his spare time at home by himself. He had hoped his mother would tell George to shut up and forget about it, but George had won out. And after that, Leo always had to be at the hotel, doing his homework or fooling around in the parking lot by himself or watching TV with the paying guests in the little lounge. He never got to see anything good. Those traveling people liked to watch the dumbest things, like those soppy programs where a little kid gets cancer or radiation burns and then in the end the people wipe their eyes (if they're women) or clear their throats (if they're men) and say it was "moving." It was usually moving all right—moving enough to make you throw up. Leo hated those dumb tearjerking programs.

He hoped Mr. Baines wasn't going to say anything about the boat almost going over. That might lead to a swimming conversation and he'd have to think hard what to say. It was bad enough that in a letter to the old man last March, thanking him for the job, he said that he liked to swim. He didn't even know why he'd said it. But now, having come within an inch of going upside down in the water, he realized that he might get caught in that lie, and that he'd better teach himself, whether he wanted to learn or not. No one wanted a liar around. He could come down here at night, after Mr. Baines went to bed, and practice. Soon he would be as good as any of them. Leo gripped the oars. He felt better already.

Leo neared the island as the old people were getting out of the guide boat, doing a lot of talking about which one was going to move first, both of them finally backing onto the dock, then rolling around and bringing their legs up until they were on all fours, and finally managing to stand up. Meanwhile, Tigger was balanced on one of those long muscular legs of his, the free foot holding the boat still against the side of the dock, his hands gripping first Miss Maudie and then Mr. Baines. After the potential crisis was over, Tigger dropped to one knee and lifted out all the picnic baskets with ease. Then he tied the painter to a hook on the side of the dock and pushed the guide boat out of the way to make room for Leo.

As Tigger cleared the dock, Leo made his approach. "Potential" was a favorite word that George used: "We've got a potential situation here where a double play could put out three men . . ." Or: "Young Sam Goodbody's got the potential for being a fine mechanic if he'd ever get out of bed." Or sometimes things like: "Leo's got the potential for thinking if he could get his mind off his stomach." Everybody would laugh then and look at Leo with his head bent over a big plate of french fries. They never even glanced his way when he was bent over a book.

Leo studied the dogs and realized he had a potential situation for disaster. They were all three standing up now and watching the dock grow closer. Leo looked over his shoulder at Louisa, who was stepping from front paw to front paw, tensed for action. Nectarine had begun to pant something awful, and even Tossie was whining to get out. With about twenty feet to go, Tossie made the first move. She stepped up onto the seat and dived off into the water with a mighty splash. Nectarine got hysterical and tried to follow, but was too timid to make a good clean leap, instead rocking the boat and whining and carrying on like a fool before she finally fell over the side. At this, Louisa raced past Leo, knocking the oar out of the oarlock and almost knocking him out of the boat. Barking hysterically, she finally got herself over the side in a frenzied white heap and hit the water, sending about a bucketful into the boat.

"Whoa!" Leo managed to get the oar back in place and the boat headed in the right direction. No one came running back onto the dock to see what had happened. The crisis was over, and he had made out pretty good. "Pretty good," as Mr. Baines would repeat.

There was a lot of commotion on the little island. Miss Maudie was yelling at the dogs and trying to grab their collars; Mr. Baines was limping up and down, pointing his crooked finger in a succession of places. Tigger was reaching under bushes pulling out bits of wrap and plastic and other debris and throwing them into the stone fireplace. Pookie was hanging back by the lean-to, her arms limp by her sides.

"There's another one!" Mr. Baines grabbed a long stick off the ground and began jabbing it under a bush.

"Tossie! Get over here! Nectarine! Drop that!" Miss Maudie clearly had her hands full.

Leo went quickly to Miss Maudie's side and took Nectarine and Tossie both by their collars. "What's happened?"

"Look at this mess! Just look at it! Louisa! Don't you touch that!" Miss Maudie managed to collar the white dog and jerk a plastic package out of its mouth. "Here! Tigger! Take this!"

"What is it?" Leo asked.

"Looks like a pork chop," Miss Maudie answered.

"Where'd it come from?"

"Part of this mess," she answered. "Whoever pic-nicked here last night left their dinner under the bushes. Here's some more lettuce," she said to Tigger.

"To hell with the lettuce," Mr. Baines replied. "It'll make compost. We've got to get up this other mess."

Leo watched, fascinated, as Tigger gathered bits of plastic, pork chops, raw potatoes, tomatoes, ears of corn, and paper napkins. He'd never seen so much wasted food. Why would anyone bring all that on a picnic and then not eat it? His mother had always said, "Take what you want on your plate, but don't leave any of it there. Waste not, want not."

"Want me to help?" he asked Tigger.

"You just hold the dogs. I've about got it all now."

"Put it all in the fireplace, Tigger," Mr. Baines said, as if Tigger weren't doing that very thing. "I'll start gathering some twigs for a good hot fire. Pookie, dar-ling, give me a hand. Let's get a lot of dry sticks."

Pookie shuffled around in a dreamlike state, occa-sionally bending to pick up a small stick and carry it to the fire.

Tigger took some newspapers from the lean-to and wadded them into the fireplace. There were dry kin-dling pieces neatly stacked by the side of the log structure, and he took a few of these and arranged them over the paper and sticks.

Mr. Baines found matches sealed in a glass jar and left on the shelf in the lean-to. He took out one and handed it to Tigger. "There. That ought to do it. Look at that confounded pile."

"The dogs can go now, Leo," Miss Maudie said, slapping her hands together as if she had been the one to grovel around in the dirt picking up trash. "I'd like to know who was here last night."

"Better not ask," Tigger said. "You might be sorry if you knew."

"Tigger's right, Maudie," Mr. Baines said. "The thing to do is mention it to Creeper and have him bring it up at the meeting. Whoever's responsible will know who he is and won't do it again. Put another piece of wood on."

Tigger added another small stick to the blazing fire. "It'll be all right this way. No point in wasting the firewood."

"It's lucky we planned on a cold picnic tonight," Miss Maudie commented as she began to unpack the baskets onto a wooden picnic table. "I'd hesitate to cook over that steaming debris."

"You sure you brought the Scotch?" Mr. Baines asked. Then he winked at Leo. "Something important like that is just the sort of thing might slip her mind."

"It was hardly possible to forget with you reminding me twenty-five times." Miss Maudie put the

Scotch bottle on the table. "Good thing everyone doesn't think Scotch is medicinal; it would get a bad name."

"You once forgot it," Mr. Baines said coolly, picking up the bottle and unscrewing the cap. "When you find the paper cups, I'll have one."

"I brought a Coke for you, Leo," Miss Maudie said. "Hope that's what you like."

"Yes, ma'am."

"Leo," Mr. Baines said, "be a good boy and get some water from the lake in one of those cups."

"Yes, sir." He followed Tigger down a narrow path to the lake and stepped onto a boulder by the shore. "Wow," he said softly, looking across the stretch of lily pads to the expanse of glassy water. "This sure is pretty."

"Sure is," Tigger answered, washing his hands on the side of the rock away from Leo. "Get the water over there where the bottom hasn't been stirred up."

Leo knelt on the rock and dipped the cup into the clear water. He looked into the cup. "It's so clear. When you're out on the lake, the water looks black, but here it's clear as can be."

"You like to fish?" Tigger asked.

"Some."

"Grandpa knows a lot about it. You'll learn things being with him." Tigger stood up and easily stepped from the rock to the little clear patch of dirt and ambled up the path.

Leo had never seen anyone built like Tigger. He was tall and very slim, but you could see those long muscles ripple when he moved. He wore blue jeans cut off just below the hips, and another of those T-shirts, this one pale blue with a white C and a small oar across it on the front.

"You find the water all right?" Mr. Baines called.

"Yes, sir. Coming." Leo scrambled back to the picnic area.

"You want to eat now or fish first, Tigger?" Miss Maudie asked.

Tigger looked past the trunks of the tall pines to the lake. "What do you think, Grandpa? Think it'll stay calm like this?"

"I think so. Shouldn't be any wind at all tonight."

"Then we can eat first." Tigger looked in a large wicker hamper and brought out a small Styrofoam case. He took out a beer.

"Want a beer or something, Pookie?" Mr. Baines asked as he leaned against the table top.

"She might have a Coke," Tigger answered, looking over at his sister.

When she didn't answer, he opened one and took it to her. She nodded and began to sip it.

"Help yourself, Leo," Miss Maudie said. "Good Lord, Ethel's sent us enough food for an army. Hope everyone's hungry."

"I am," Tigger said, sitting beside his grandfather on the bench part of the table.

Mr. Baines chuckled and looked at Leo. "Ethel's the cook at the dining room. She likes to keep full stomachs."

"You didn't cook this?" Leo asked Miss Maudie as he opened a Coke.

"No, I do lunch and that's all. Ethel feeds us at night, whether we eat in or out."

Mr. Baines elaborated. "Sometimes she sends steaks or hamburgers or chops or other things to cook out on the fireplace. But if you tell her you don't want to cook, she does it all in the kitchen and sends it ready to eat. It's good either way. Wait till you taste her cherry pie."

"We have chocolate cake tonight," Miss Maudie said. "Louisa! Get over here! She'll just exhaust herself chasing that bird."

"Good," Mr. Baines replied. "Then she might try sleeping."

Leo agreed with him. If she slept the whole way back to the boat house, he wouldn't mind. And Nectarine, too. He looked around for Tossie. "Where's Tossie?" he asked.

"Oh, she'll be in the water somewhere chasing sunfish," Miss Maudie said.

"Does she ever catch them?" Leo asked.

"Of course not," Miss Maudie snapped.

Leo hastily took a swallow of Coke. That was a dumb thing to have said.

"The fact is," Mr. Baines said to Miss Maudie, "you don't know whether she does or not. You don't watch her the whole time. Just put a little splash of Scotch in that, will you, Tigger, my boy. I put in too much water."

"Did Ethel send us cheese and crackers?" Tigger asked.

"Coming up," Miss Maudie answered, unwrapping a big chunk of pale golden cheese. "This local cheddar she gets is better every year. Here you go." She pushed a paper plate with the cheese and a knife on it to Tigger, then handed him a box of crackers. "Maybe you can get Pookie to eat one."

Tigger cut slices of cheese and put them on crackers. He offered them to the old people first, then to Leo, who gratefully took one. Then Tigger ate one himself as he stood up and walked over to Pookie. "Want it?"

Pookie took the cracker and sat on the log at the front of the lean-to. She smiled at Tigger, holding the cracker on the palm of her hand.

Tigger went back to the table and fixed himself another one. "Everybody's on their own now." He pushed the plate to the middle of the table.

Leo wanted about six, but hung back, again looking out at the lake. "It sure is pretty." He turned to Pookie. He'd like to go sit by her, but that might be too familiar for the first day. "You want anything?" he asked, walking over in her direction.

She raised her head and squinted her eyes at him. "What?"

"I said, can I get you something?"

"No," she said, letting her eyelids slide shut.

Leo stared at her. Maybe she *was* sick—but why didn't Tigger and the old people notice? He took a step nearer her. "You all right?" he asked.

Pookie opened her eyes.

Leo could see they weren't focusing on him, though she looked in his direction.

"Pookie?"

"Go away," she said in a low toneless voice. "Leave me alone."

Leo recoiled, reddening, feeling an instant hurt. He quickly turned toward the lake. What a fool he was. Right off, he had gone too far, and look at the rebuff he'd received. His mother was right when she'd said, "Those people in at the club have been raised differently from us. You're not one of them and probably won't understand their ways. Be careful how you step."

He walked back toward the others.

There were two picnic tables, and Miss Maudie arranged the food on the farther one, leaving the one where they were sitting for the drinks and empty baskets.

Leo almost forgot about Pookie as he saw Miss

Maudie unwrap the packages of food. Cold fried chicken, stuffed eggs, bowls of potato salad and cole slaw, slices of ham rolled around melon strips, a bag of cookies, half a chocolate cake, and things like butter and jam and pickles. "I'll just leave these biscuits wrapped up in the tea towel to keep warm," Miss Maudie said. "The rest is cold. Now anytime you want to eat, it's ready. Nectarine! Get your paws off the table!"

"Sit down, Miss Maudie, and relax," Mr. Baines said. "We'll have some more cheese and crackers with our drinks. Help yourself, Leo. Now, Tigger, reach into that little chest and get me another piece of ice. Thank you, my boy. It's going to be a fine night for fishing. Not a breath of wind. Just the way it should be. You come from a fishing family, Leo?"

"Yes, sir. My daddy used to fish a lot and my mother likes it, too. I haven't done much myself lately."

"What kind of fishing did your daddy do?" Mr. Baines asked.

Leo looked away. "All kinds," he answered, as he caught a glimpse of the small black loon's head way out across the water. "Look, there's the loon." He wanted to change the subject. He didn't want Mr. Baines to ask him what kind of rod his daddy had used or what kind of boat he had had.

"That other small island over there in the West Bay

of the lake is where the loons nest every year." Miss Maudie said this with authority. "They've been coming here as long as I can remember."

"That whole side over there is called West Bay," Mr. Baines said. "This lake's shaped sort of like a horseshoe. Just look at all that food. I'm beginning to build up an appetite. Maybe we have time for some more of that good cheese. Just put a tad of Scotch in that cup, will you, Tigger. We'll get the right balance here yet."

The pungent aroma of the searing chops and potatoes and corn was really getting to Leo. He drank the rest of his Coke to fill up his empty stomach. His meager lunch hadn't lasted long at all. He longed to cut some cheese and put it on a cracker or two, but he hesitated. He didn't know whether to fix crackers for everyone, as Tigger had done, or just fix himself one and get out of the way. If he cut a lot of cheese and no one wanted any more, then it would look as if he were wasting it. He decided to just forget the cheese. There was plenty of chicken, and he was going to get his sights on a big piece right from the beginning.

"Well, I think I'll have a piece of cheese on a cracker," Mr. Baines said. "Anyone else?"

Miss Maudie pointed a finger at her brother. "Don't eat so much of that—you'll spoil your appetite," she warned.

Ignoring her, Mr. Baines slowly cut a big chunk of

cheese and took a bite off it before he put the rest on a cracker.

"This is pretty good," Mr. Baines said. "Pretty good."

Leo couldn't remember when he had ever eaten so much—except that time after the church pancake supper. At the end of the first week he could hardly get his blue jeans to stay shut over his stomach. He knew the khakis would hook around better, but he sure wasn't going to wear them. Pookie had already called him "Highpockets" two more times without any reminding. "Hi, Highpockets, have you seen Grandpa?" and that with the old man sitting not ten feet away. And the other time was right out on the lake: she leaned over the side of the canoe and said, "Look, there's Highpockets," and just about tipped herself and the canoe over. Tigger had to yell at her to sit up.

Leo looked down at his blue jeans and wondered how they'd look if he cut them off the way Tigger had cut his. He felt like a jerk going around in long pants when all the young people in here wore shorts. Except Pookie, who seemed to have a whole drawer full of shrunken long underwear.

Of course, his mother would probably kill him if he cut up his pants. He could hear George now: "Go out and buy long pants so you can cut off two thirds of them to decorate the dump. Now that's taking care of money." No, it wouldn't be worth it.

Leo had noticed right off that there was a dress code in the club and it seemed to go by age. The high school and college crowd pretty much dressed like Tigger, cool-looking and real casual-like in crew shirts or T-shirts stamped with the names of their schools. At night, when the air turned chilly, they wore regular blue jeans and sweat shirts. Their mothers worked real hard at being youthful-looking, wearing little skimpy tight-fitting tops, usually white, over real short white shorts. They played a lot of tennis or sat around getting tan. Miss Maudie said they were ruining their skin and would look like Egyptian mummies by the time they were fifty. The old people usually wore khaki pants and cotton plaid shirts and some kind of fishing-type hat on their heads, the same for the men and the women. You could see people half a mile off and tell how old they were by the way they dressed.

Leo's mother wore all sorts of different things. She was real neat and always spotlessly clean; she often got up before breakfast to iron her clothes. Sometimes she wore a regular cotton dress for waiting tables, sometimes a skirt and white blouse. She had a blue-jeans skirt she wore on Saturdays. And if they went to the lake on her day off to picnic, she wore slacks or shorts, depending on the weather. Leo had always thought she dressed real nice, but now he realized she probably looked pretty corny. She was so different from the people in here.

His mother wouldn't be able to believe her eyes if she saw Pookie's clothes. She'd probably say: "That child needs help. Just looking the other way's not going to pull her through."

As Leo sat on the steps of the porch and stared at the grass, waiting for Mr. Baines to wake up from his nap, Pookie slid out the door and crept along the porch, oblivious to Leo's presence. When she turned the corner of the house, Leo jumped up and quietly followed her. He stopped at the corner, leaned into the log siding, and stealthily poked his head around the building.

Pookie stood at the railing, not looking out but staring at something in her hand. She did this for a long time, then hunched over, cradling her hands to her chest, and gingerly backed to the big wooden chair. When her leg touched, she sat on the edge and began fiddling with whatever it was in her hands. A little wisp of smoke appeared, and Pookie bent her head into her hands.

Leo's lips parted, but he was speechless. There was

no question in his mind what Pookie was inhaling. She didn't have a stomach problem or any other natural phenomenon. Pookie was a druggie.

He'd seen kids in town hanging around the hotel getting stoned, outside the hotel on grass and inside at the bar on too much beer, and now he wondered why he hadn't recognized the symptoms in Pookie from the beginning.

George said he never minded the kids coming into the hotel for a beer or a Coke or something. He said he'd rather have them in there at the hotel than out at some honky-tonk and up to no good. As long as they were in the hotel, he could keep an eye on them, and if they started to get bombed or something, he could get them into a conversation and turn their heads away from their drinks. Sometimes it worked; sometimes it didn't. But at least he tried. Plenty of times they left the hotel and just stood in the parking lot smoking grass and drinking out of a bottle hidden in a paper bag. George left them alone then. "They're in the Lord's hands when they walk out of here, and this is something He's got to fix."

Leo watched Pookie, dipping her head into her hands, leaning back and staring into the air, finally folding herself back into the chair like a butterfly melding into a tree limb.

He pulled back on hearing a noise behind him and looked around the corner to see Mr. Baines at the screen door. Leo hurried quietly toward him.

Leo and Mr. Baines usually went fishing in the afternoons, unless Mr. Baines's arthritis was acting up, and then they sat around in the sun or by the fire if it was damp, drinking iced tea and sorting out trout flies. Of course, Leo had to slip a little Scotch in Mr. Baines's iced tea when Miss Maudie wasn't looking, but that was easy so far. She was always preoccupied with the dogs or playing bridge with three of her "cronies," as Mr. Baines called them.

"Just put a splash in this, Leo," Mr. Baines would say. Or: "Let's have some iced tea with a stick in it." Leo knew what he was talking about and would slip into the linen closet and reach for the hidden bottle. And every day there seemed to be a full one there waiting. Leo had never seen the old man stowing one away, but he knew he did. Sure couldn't have been during the night, because Leo's room was right next to Mr. Baines's, and the snoring that came from it during the night was like being back at the sawmill where his daddy had worked.

"Leo, I just remembered something," Mr. Baines said as he shuffled across the porch with his usual amount of noise. "We never followed up to make sure Miss Maudie spoke to Creeper McGraw about that mess at Mink Island. Do you think she remembered?"

"Yes, sir." Miss Maudie had a mind like a steel trap. She never forgot anything.

"You're probably right, but maybe we ought to go see him about it, too. What do you think?"

"If you say so."

"I think we probably should. I want to make damn sure he brings it up at the annual meeting; in the meantime he can pass the word around, and we'll hope most people will hear it. Maybe we should have a driving lesson."

"Here? On the clearing?" His heart began to race.

"Why not? You're getting to be pretty good. Pretty good."

Leo got the Jeep started and even into first gear without stripping out the clutch, but he was so nervous that he took his foot off the clutch too soon and they jerked to a halt.

"Now just ease up on it," the old man said, not looking to left or right, his head jutted forward from his shirt.

Leo glanced nervously at him, then started again. This time he managed to lurch forward, and they began to rumble up the road.

"Now shift into second."

Leo did that all right, and they picked up a little speed. He got the Jeep up the road to the corner, where the main dirt road intersected theirs, and was about to turn toward the clubhouse when Beek came bouncing around the corner at a run.

"Hold on, Leo. Hello there, Beek, darling!" Mr. Baines waved his bony hand out the window.

Leo slammed on the brakes and the engine stalled. Now why did she have to be coming, just when he was getting good? He stepped on the clutch and got the gear back into first. He'd have to start all over now.

Beek waved and jogged on by.

"Great girl. She's out running almost as much as Tigger is. Let's go." Mr. Baines put his head back in his staring-ahead position.

Leo had seen Tigger rowing a lot, both his red canoe and that long racing shell he had brought from Princeton to use for the summer, but he hadn't seen him doing much running. He watched Beek going away from them, down the road toward Mink Pond. She ran in long easy strides. Boy, she sure was tall for a girl. And that blond hair of hers was so light it was almost white. She had it cut real short, and as best Leo could determine the few times he had seen her, she never combed it. It was just a lot of crinkly strands that stood out all over. She was a rower, too, on the girls' crew at Princeton.

"Beek's some athlete," Mr. Baines said. "Smart, too. She was accepted at every place she applied. Glad she picked Princeton. She and Tigger are quite a pair. We just going to sit here?"

Leo got started again and even managed to turn the corner before they had another interruption.

"Stop." Mr. Baines leaned out the window. "Creeper! Come here a minute, Creeper!"

This time Leo got his foot on the clutch before he stopped, and the engine idled as they waited for Creeper McGraw to come loping down the bank onto the road. Boy, Creeper was even taller than Tigger.

Creeper nodded at Leo. "How you doing, Mr. Baines?"

"Now, Creeper, did Miss Maudie speak to you about the condition of the picnic site at Mink?"

"She sure did, and I'm real sorry that happened."

"We just can't have that sort of thing, Creeper. I know you've got your hands full, trying to run this place and not drive us into bankruptcy, but there's just got to be more attention paid to the picnic sites. If someone takes something into the woods, they can bring it out just as easily. There's no excuse in leaving a mess behind. Now don't you think someone could supervise all this and make sure this sort of thing doesn't happen?"

"Mr. Baines, I've been thinking: we need a committee to oversee the picnic areas, the lean-tos, firewood by the fireplaces, all that sort of thing. And I think the person to head this committee should be you."

"Me?"

"Yes, sir, you. You could make the rounds while you're on the lakes fishing. Stop by the islands or wherever there's a lean-to and a fireplace and check things out—you know, firewood, axes, paper, matches, sleeping conditions, docks, all that. You spend more time on the lakes than anyone here, and you're the logical person. Also you're the ideal person because you really care and you'll pay attention and not forget. You could get two other people to be on the committee with you. What do you say?"

"Why, I'd be honored. Leo and I can make the rounds, as you say, whenever we're on a lake. Now do you have any suggestions about who you'd like to serve with us?"

"No, sir. You just pick whomever you want. I've got to run now. I got myself signed up for mixed doubles this afternoon. I'll make sure the tennis courts are cleaned up. You take care of the picnic sites. If anything's needed at the sites, you tell me or Rastus, and we'll take care of it." He nodded and loped off.

Mr. Baines leaned back against the seat, and a big grin appeared on his face. "Well, well, looks like we've got us a job, Leo. Think we can handle it?"

Leo smiled. "Yes, sir. We sure can." He was glad Mr. Baines looked so happy. It made him feel so good he forgot to be nervous. He started the Jeep up just like a pro, and they began to cruise around the clearing at ten miles an hour, churning up one road and down another.

"There's Peggy Maitland. Didn't know she'd arrived. She and my daughter were the same age. Grew up together. Great girl. Hello there, Peggy, darling! Now she'd be a good one on our committee. I don't like the sound of 'picnic committee.' We'll call it the 'lean-to committee.' That sounds better. And after all, the lean-tos are the biggest things at the sites. Yes, sir, the lean-to committee. Peggy Maitland would be a good member. We'll have to think of someone else."

"How about Miss Maudie?"

"That's a pretty good idea. Pretty good."

Leo ground down the road toward their cottage, which looked like a big fortress from up the road. He had made a good suggestion and he had handled the Jeep well. He almost felt that he belonged at the club. Someday, maybe, he'd go to a big college like Princeton, leaving George and the hotel behind. Of course, he'd miss his mother, but she could always come visit him wherever he was.

"You did real well, Leo. In no time you'll be an expert." Mr. Baines pulled his knees up with his gnarled hands and struggled to get sideways and out the door.

Leo jumped out of the Jeep and ran around to Mr. Baines's side. He put out his hand, and the old man clutched it and steadied himself. "It's hell to get old, Leo. But I guess I'm still useful."

"Yes, sir. You sure are." Leo nodded and watched Mr. Baines straighten up his hunched-over back as best he could and go up the steps to the porch with a real springy walk.

"Maudie! Where are you, Maudie? I've got some news for you."

Leo followed, smiling.

"What's Grandpa so happy about?" Tigger asked Leo. "He catch a four-pound trout out of Split Rock Pond?"

Leo had stopped by the kitchen to eat a few cookies. The big jar on the table by the window was always full. Miss Maudie got Ethel to bake a fresh batch for her three times a week: sometimes chocolate chips, sometimes ginger snaps or molasses crisps, sometimes plain sugar cookies. Leo's favorites were the ones with raspberry filling. No one in this family liked the peanut-butter ones, so that was out. Leo liked peanut-butter cookies and always tried to sneak a few when they were up at the dining room, where Ethel put out a plate of assorted ones for lunch and dinner.

"Mr. McGraw wants him to head a lean-to committee and make sure the picnic sites are cleaned up and well-stocked with supplies."

"That should have made him happy. You going fishing now?"

Leo shrugged. "Probably, but I'm not sure. It's getting kind of late."

"If he gets involved talking, you and I could go down to Beaver and try to pick up a bass or two."

Leo's heart swelled. He couldn't believe that Tigger

was actually asking him to go fishing with him. He tried to act calm. "Sure. That sounds good." He suppressed a big grin. "You could give me some pointers."

"You won't learn much from me. 'Look over there!' is not an expression I use!" He laughed, reaching past Leo for a cooky. " 'Look over there!' Grandpa's been saying that since I can remember. We were raised on that phrase. I guess you're getting your fill of it, too."

Leo smiled. "I don't mind. He always points out something interesting. I've seen a lot of things I never would have seen."

"Leo! Leo!" Mr. Baines called from the hall. "Oh, there you are," he said, limping into the kitchen. "You going to stand here eating cookies with Tigger or are you going to get in an hour's fishing with me?"

"You better get going," Tigger said to Leo. "Time and Grandpa wait for no man."

"You coming with us, Tigger, my boy?" Mr. Baines asked.

Tigger hesitated, then said, "Well, I guess not, now that I think about it. I'll try to repair that broken canoe seat before dinner."

"Good," Mr. Baines said, heading for the door. "No point in having a canoe out of commission. Bring a handful of those cookies, Leo, for both of us."

Leo grabbed four cookies and followed Mr. Baines.

Leo sat in the living room waiting for Mr. Baines to go upstairs to bed. He had already made up his mind that this was the night he was going to begin his swimming lessons. But he had to wait for Mr. Baines to get settled in for the night and begin his snoring. Then he could slip down to the lake unseen.

It was after nine and had already gotten dark. Mr. Baines liked to sit on the porch and watch the sunset spread across the western sky. "See those golds, pinks, and reds that always come in the northern mountains?" he'd ask Leo. "Watch how quickly the colors change. Those new hues blend in very subtly. Now look over there!" Leo watched as the sun sank farther behind the dark mountain silhouettes. "Here's where the violets ease out the golds," Mr. Baines said excitedly. "And see how they finally turn into a deepening blue." He paused, then said, "And darkness finally comes." Some nights Mr. Baines liked to comment on each color. Other nights he sat and watched in silence. But he always ended by saying "That was a pretty good show. Pretty good."

Leo looked around the big room. He knew the dark ceiling was black cherry, the walls were tongue-and-groove hard maple, and the staircase railing and posts were walnut, because Mr. Baines had told him that and how all the wood in the cottages was milled "right down there on Mink Outlet at the old sawmill by those old-timers who sure knew how to turn out a fine product. Nowadays people don't take pride in their work. But back then, they settled for nothing less than perfection. Just look at this woodwork." And Leo had to agree with him: it was fine work. He guessed that if his daddy had lived and had put his mind to it, he could have turned out a fine product like this, too. Of course, the kind of mill work he had done was mostly for a lumber company. But he could have done this fancy work if he had wanted to.

And just look at all the rest of the stuff in this room! There was a big wicker wing chair in the corner, next to a table with a lamp that had a green glass shade on it. There was a tall grandfather's clock in another corner and a real long table stretched beneath the stairs, holding books, magazines, and maps. Then there were easy chairs with soft cushions, and two big sofas. Miss Maudie said it was a hodgepodge of styles, but that didn't matter to her. She said she liked good pieces and she liked comfortable pieces, and she saw no reason why you couldn't throw them all in together. Leo thought they looked fine. He thought the whole room was fine, including all the books in the bookcases.

He looked up at the deer heads on the walls. Sometimes just the skulls with the antlers were mounted. He knew several of them belonged to Tigger, who had shot them when he was up here for Thanksgiving vacations. There was one bear head mounted on a plaque, a skin of a lynx stretched next to the bookcases, and two fish skins mounted on a blue board. And in between all these things were old photographs of women in long skirts and men with fishing rods who looked as if they'd just stepped out of an office, dressed in their jackets, city hats, and ties.

Leo wondered what it would be like to come here for Thanksgiving vacation. He bet there'd be a lot of people, gathering in the evenings, having a good time, telling what they'd seen in the woods, lighting a fire in that big fireplace that took four-foot logs, getting Ethel to come in and cook roasts and pies and hot breads and turkey.

"Leo."

"Sir?" Leo jumped to his feet.

"Give me a hand, will you?" Mr. Baines handed him a stack of newspapers. "You take these, and I can free my hands."

Leo took the papers and followed the old man to the

staircase. If he read all these papers, Leo wouldn't get out of the house before daybreak.

"You going to read all these?" he asked.

Mr. Baines got a leg up on the first step and grabbed the railing with both hands. "I doubt it." He pulled himself up, step by step, Leo right behind and on the ready in case the old man stumbled and fell back. "Must be going to rain," Mr. Baines said. "I'm feeling pretty stiff tonight."

"Nonsense," Miss Maudie retorted from the doorway. "You just did too much today. The weather's going to be fine tomorrow."

Mr. Baines stopped and chuckled. He shook his head from side to side. "Well, she'll probably be right. She usually is."

The three dogs suddenly raced past Leo and Mr. Baines, snapping and barking and knocking into each other. They turned the corner at the top of the stairs and crashed into a table near the upstairs sitting room.

Leo held his breath, ready to drop the papers and grab the old man, who now was tottering around on the step, his bony arthritic fingers clutching at the railing.

"Watch out!" He hunched over the railing and steadied himself. "Damned dogs! Maudie! Why can't you control those damned dogs?"

"You should have waited for them to go first," she answered. "You knew they were ready to go up."

"Well, did they know I was ready to go up, too?" he asked.

"I have no idea," she said. "You've got to be the one to watch out."

Mr. Baines began his slow progress again. "Careful, Leo, in case they decide to come back down again."

They finally made it to the top and into Mr. Baines's bedroom. Leo put the newspapers on the big bedside table, already chockablock with books, *Field & Stream*, *Fly Fisherman*, writing pads, pencils, scraps of yellowing paper that had been there a long time, judging by the color, and a variety of pill bottles.

Leo then went back through the upstairs sitting room to the big bathroom at the end of the hall to fill the water pitcher. He carried this back and put it on the table with everything else.

Mr. Baines was sitting on the side of the bed with his pants leg pulled up, all hunched over and trying to reach his shoe.

Leo squatted down and untied the shoelace. Not that that would do any good, with that brace still hooked under the instep and going up both sides of the old man's leg.

"Want some help with that brace?" Leo asked.

"We'll see." Mr. Baines began unhooking the catches at the top of the steel brace. "Damned thing gets stiffer all the time. Maybe these hinges need oiling."

Leo watched. More than likely those hinges were

fine, and it was the twisted fingers that were getting stiffer. That first night, when he was helping Mr. Baines get everything he'd need, the old man had told him he'd had an accident playing polo when he was a young man, and the leg never had healed right. Now he had bad arthritis in it and had to wear a brace.

"There, about got it," Mr. Baines grunted.

Leo hadn't known anything about polo, but the next day he'd seen a book in the living room about it, and he'd read enough of it to learn that it was a pretty rough sport played by rich people. You had to be rich to own a polo pony, just for starters. There were pictures of the players all dressed up in white shirts and pants and high leather boots, standing in front of a big fancy clubhouse, and then pictures of the men on their ponies (they never called them "horses"), galloping down a field with their long-handled mallets readied to hit the ball. They all looked rich. And Leo sure could see how you'd smash up your leg if it got in the way of a mallet, or if the pony fell on top of you, or even if you just fell off and got trampled. He hadn't asked for the details. Things like that made him sick.

"Got it." Mr. Baines let the brace fall to the floor; then he shook his foot and kicked the shoe off.

Leo picked up the heavy steel brace and laid it across a chair; then he picked up the shoe and put it under the bedside table. "You got everything you want?" he asked.

"I think I do," Mr. Baines said, looking around at

the bed and table. "Just pull down that shade for me, and you can go to bed yourself. You must be tired."

"I'm sort of tired." He was beginning to feel really keyed up at the prospect of sneaking down to Mink without being seen. "You all set?"

"Yes, I am. Good night, Leo. And don't let me oversleep."

"No, sir." That was the last thing the old man said every night. Actually, he was usually awake before Leo. Every morning Leo could hear him clumping down the hall to the bathroom about an hour before Leo got up.

Leo went next door to his own bedroom. There was a connecting door between the two rooms, and supposedly Leo could hear Mr. Baines calling for help if he needed it. So far he'd snored right through every night, and the only getting up Leo had done was to get another pillow to put over his ears.

Leo stretched out on his bed to wait until the snoring began. He was wide awake and ready to go, his heart thumping with excitement.

Leo stayed on his bed until he was sure Mr. Baines was sound asleep. Then he went down to the living room and picked up a magazine and stood by the long table beneath the stairs, flipping through the pages, listening for the slightest sound. Next he went outside and lingered on the porch, trembling in the night air, and again listened. Then he quietly slipped down the steps, and, making sure he stayed on the grass and away from the gravel, he moved silently and quickly up the road to the corner where it joined the main club road. Here he paused again and listened.

Lights burned in many of the cottage windows, and he could hear muffled sounds of laughter and an occasional dog barking. He had figured Tigger was probably up at Beek's house as usual, playing cards, but he had no idea where Pookie went after dinner or when she came home. Most nights her bedroom door was shut when he and Mr. Baines went up, so he assumed she'd gone to bed. No one could hear her anyway. She was like a shadow moving across the floor.

And now he became a shadow himself, going silently and swiftly down the road beneath the strip of open sky that snaked a path through the woods spreading out on both sides of him. Soon he caught sight of the lake glistening in the moonlight through the trees, and in no time he stood at the water's edge, looking out across the silvery expanse.

He shivered. The mountain air became cold when the sun sank behind the western ridges. He drew his arms in close to his body and put his hands up around his shoulders. Maybe it was too cold. Maybe it would be warmer another night.

"No," he said to himself, "I'm going to do it." He looked along the edge of the shore, trying to figure out the best place to go in. His gaze swept past the main boat house and on to the dock below the canoes, all lined up along the gently sloping bank like sleeping giants. That would be a good place. He could wade out beside the dock and even swim back and forth at the end of the dock. That way, if he got a leg cramp or a lungful of water, he could reach for the dock and hang on. It was always good to have a plan in case of disaster.

He shivered again and pushed the word "disaster" from his mind. Stepping as quietly as he could over the roots and spongy leaves that blanketed the ground on either side of the boat house, he went up the bank to the trail of pine needles that led to the canoe house and dock. The woods were filled with the rich smells of decaying old growth and the sweetness of new summer plants. Leo couldn't identify any of the strange aromas, but he took a deep breath and wished he could say with authority: moose-maple leaves, bunchberries in bloom, water lilies and the pickerel-weed flowers, hemlock, white pine—things he had heard his daddy talk about. There were animal smells that lingered, too: perhaps they were big deer and fawn, beaver in the lake, black bear.

He slowly turned his head and looked all around. There could be a black bear here, standing still just watching him and waiting to see what he was going to do. Quickly, he took off his shirt and draped it over the nearest canoe. Boy, it was cold. He bent down to untie his sneakers.

"Hi, Highpockets."

"Yow!" Leo jumped about three feet straight up into the air, and when he came down his heart stayed up in his throat.

"It's all right," the slight small voice said. "I didn't mean to frighten you."

Leo grabbed for his shirt and fumbled his arms into it. He was shaking violently now. Where was she? His eyes were opened in big wide circles, and he searched the area around the canoes and beside the dock.

"Are you going swimming?"

He began to shake his head. His teeth were chattering so loudly he'd never be able to get any words past them to be heard. He quickly put his hand over his mouth and pressed it. By the time he got his teeth under control, his shoulders weren't shaking quite so much. He pushed his shirttail into his blue jeans. "Where are you?"

"Here."

He finally saw her, slid down beside a pale-colored canoe where her long underwear blended into the metal, like part of a design. "What are you doing, Pookie?" he asked.

"Sitting," she answered softly. "There's plenty of room. Unless you're going to swim first."

"No, I don't think I'll swim after all. It's pretty cold." He threaded his way between two canoes toward the water's edge. He now saw that her legs were stuck out in front of her, but they blended into the sand. He could see the tiny glow of a joint in her fingers.

"Do you want to sit down?" she asked.

Leo sat down and leaned against the next canoe. He looked at Pookie. There was enough moonlight to see that dreamy faraway look on her face. Yet her voice was pretty clear.

"You come here often?" he asked.

She nodded.

"I mean, after dinner, at night, *alone*."

Again she nodded.

"You aren't scared?"

There was a long pause, so long that Leo thought she must not have heard him; then she said quietly, "Sometimes."

"How come you sit here by yourself then?"

She shook her head. "Where else should I go?"

"I don't know."

"You want this for a while?" she asked, offering him the joint.

"Oh, no thanks." Leo turned away, embarrassed. He didn't want her to think he was too much of a baby, but heck—he didn't want to get fuzzy-headed on pot. He hated seeing her with it in her skinny little fingers. "How come you need that?" he blurted out without thinking.

"It helps," she said, and her head sank a little onto her chest.

For an awful moment, Leo thought she was going to cry. Boy, he hated it when girls cried. But she didn't. She just stared down into the sand between her legs. "Yeah?" he queried.

She nodded and raised her head and stared out across the lake.

"It makes you feel better?" he asked. She probably thought he was square anyway, so he might as well go ahead and ask.

"I don't think so," she answered slowly. "I never remember how I feel."

"Then what does it do?"

"It makes me forget."

An owl called in mournful hoots in the woods and was answered by another across the lake. The far-off sounds of twigs snapping announced the approach of animals walking to the water's edge. And in the distance, the faint yipping cries of night-prowling coyotes were heard.

"Do you want to forget?" Leo finally asked.

"I guess it's the same as not wanting to remember." Pookie turned her head and looked at him, then looked away. "There's nothing I want to remember or think about."

"Must be something."

She smiled sadly. "I like things that happen and I can think about them right away. I don't like remembering yesterday. Or last year."

"Well, I guess I know what you mean. There're a lot of things I don't like to remember. But it would scare me if I forgot."

"It would?" she asked.

"Sure it would. I mean, like the time my daddy was killed—it's nothing I like to remember. But I sure wouldn't want to forget it or him."

Pookie put the joint to her lips and inhaled. She leaned her head against the canoe and slowly let out her breath. "I want to forget it all," she slowly said. "Our father went off, and we never hear a word from him, not even at Christmas."

"Not even at Christmas?"

She shook her head, rolling it from side to side on the canoe. "No. And I hate it for Tigger. Tigger would want him to be at all the races and watch him row, but no one's there, except sometimes Grandpa. He comes when he can. But our father doesn't. And we never see very much of our mother because she lives in Mexico, and it's too far off for her to be around except at Thanksgiving. And then she just comes up here for a few days, and the rest of the time she stays in the city so she can go to museums and galleries and plays and buy clothes."

"Wow." Leo thought that was terrible. "It would be pretty bad to have a daddy and not see him. You're lucky to have Mr. Baines for a grandfather."

"We know."

"My grandfather died, too. I just have my mother, and I see a lot of her, even though she's busy most of the time. But at least she's there. I would hate it if she lived in Mexico. I bet you're glad you have Miss Maudie for an aunt. I guess she's your great-aunt."

"Yes. We're lucky to have her, too."

"But they're kind of old, and they probably don't get around to seeing you as much as they should, you being away in school and all."

"That's why we spend the whole summer here. To be with them." She paused. "It's more for them, you know. They miss my mother, too, and they want some family around. I don't care where I am."

"But Tigger likes it here. I mean, he fishes and rows and all that."

"He'll graduate next spring. Then he'll have to do something else, like get a job or something."

"Wow," he said softly again. What would the old people do without him? "You'll still be here, though."

She nodded. "I guess so. There's no place else."

"Do you ever go to Mexico to visit your mother?"

Pookie's eyelids began to droop, as if all the words had drained away bits of energy. She was beginning to fade. "I never think about it."

The owls called to each other again.

"You walk down here all by yourself?" Leo asked, touching her arm to get her attention.

She nodded. "It's not so far. You walked, didn't you?"

"Yeah. But I'm not a girl."

"Boys can get scared, too." She slowly nodded her head.

"I guess." There were plenty of times Leo was scared. After his daddy was killed and his mother would be over at the hotel, leaving him all alone, he'd get scared. Once he sat right in the dark hallway, by the front door, ready to bolt through it if anyone came poking around the bushes by the windows. He sat there until midnight, when his mother came home. Then he had run to his bed and pulled the covers up and sounded all sleepy when she stuck her head in to see if he was all right. It was plenty scary being alone at night.

"Tigger ever come with you?"

"No. He plays cards and games with the others."

"You don't like to do that?" Leo thought it would probably be fun.

"No. I just like to sit down here by myself and forget."

"I'm sorry if I'm in your way," Leo said, half rising.

"Oh, no." Pookie put out her hand and stopped him. "Don't go. It's nice having someone to talk to."

"Sure?"

"Sure." She nodded. "I forget that I'm alone. But if someone's here, like you are now, then I remember, and it's very lonely when they go."

Leo knew what she meant.

"You were going to go swimming," Pookie said. "I've messed that up for you."

Leo thought about lying. He could say he'd come down here for a few fast laps before going to bed, just a race to the island and back. Something like that. Instead he said, "Actually, I'm not a very good swimmer, and I wanted to come down and practice a little. I don't want anyone to know, though."

"Don't worry, I'll forget . . ." she said, slowly nodding. Then she just closed her eyes and said nothing more.

"Maybe we ought to go back," Leo said reluctantly. "You're going to catch a cold sitting down here."

"Don't catch many colds," she said quietly.

Leo could hardly hear her. Swimming would have to wait. But he'd better think of something fast and get her out of here while he could still maneuver her up the hill. He sure wouldn't be able to carry her. And if he went for help, he would have a lot of explaining to do. "Want to go back?"

"Back?" She opened her eyes and turned them to him. She squinted.

"Yeah. Back to the house. I'm sort of cold, and you must be, too."

"You go," she whispered.

Leo looked around. If the house were on the other side of the lake, he could manage to get her in a canoe and row her home. But it was up that heart-attack hill and almost a mile to boot. "I'm not going without you," he said, crossing his fingers and hoping she would get up.

Her head rolled to one side.

"Okay? You ready?" He sat forward. She was out of it. Zonked. "Pookie? Pookie?"

She moved and looked at him.

"Let's go, Pookie. I really want to go." He was beginning to feel the urgency of the situation. Much longer, and she would be immovable altogether, with or without his help. How did she manage other nights? Did she just crawl under a canoe and fall asleep, and sometime later, near dawn, come to and walk home? "Pookie?" He poked her arm.

She smiled and whispered, "Hi."

Leo stared at her. This situation had the potential of a real nightmare. He had to think of something drastic. "Pookie? Can you hear me?"

She nodded.

Good, Leo thought. Here it comes. "I want to go back, but I'm afraid to go by myself. Will you come with me?" He held his breath and waited.

Pookie frowned; then she struggled forward. "I'll help you." She even got her voice above a whisper.

Leo stood up and pulled her to her feet. "Come on."

He took her hand and led her along the path to the dirt road, and then they began the climb home, slowly stepping on the loose gravel, Leo carefully guiding her around the rocks that protruded from the packed road.

Leo had forgotten all about why he ever came down the road. He just knew he had to get her safely home.

Leo and Mr. Baines were out on the water early the next morning. Leo was still half asleep, having been awake most of the night worrying about how his swimming was ever going to improve if Pookie was at the lake every night. And he was worried about Pookie, too. She had about everything money could buy, and it had never occurred to him that she could be so unhappy.

Leo had driven the Jeep across the Pigpen Trail to Split Rock Pond, and now they were cruising around the shore, Mr. Baines casting into the sheep-laurel bushes that hung over the water, making the fuzzy hair-bug touch lightly on the branch ends before gently dropping onto the water. "Just the way a fool frog would do it, and *bang!* If there's a bass lurking around in those shallows, he'll go for it every time. Get us in a little closer, Leo."

If they were in close, Mr. Baines said, "Get us out a little, Leo." And if they were out, he said, "Get us in a little closer, Leo." They rarely were in the right place for long.

"Yes, sir." No wonder Pookie slept until noon every day, Leo thought, pulling on the oars. Someone ought to try to help her. Did Tigger know and, for some reason that Leo didn't understand, do nothing about it? Or maybe he *had* tried and just couldn't get to first base.

"You have your mind on something else, Leo. You can't seem to keep us in the right place for very long."

Leo felt his face turn red. He looked away, over his shoulder, across the lake to the big boulder that was cleft in half and protruding from the shallow water near the point. "I was just thinking about checking up on the lean-to. We haven't inspected this one for a while."

"Now, that's a pretty good idea. Just head in that direction. But keep us this distance out from shore. We're about to go over a hot spot."

Just about every place in the lake was a "hot spot" to Mr. Baines. He'd say, "Now take us over that rock ledge real slow, Leo. It's a hot spot." And when they'd gone way past it, he'd say, "Don't know why we didn't snare one there. It's one of the best hot spots in the lake." Leo smiled. Here they were, drifting along the lake about fifty feet out from shore, sliding over hot spots too innumerable to count, and still they didn't have any fish.

"They just aren't feeding, are they?" Mr. Baines

raised his rod and with a flick of his wrist sent the line looping back behind him and then, with another flick, let it sail out in front, sending the bug to land lightly on a twig, then drop into the water.

Leo wished he could cast like that. Being expert fly fishermen was another advantage these people at the club had.

"I suppose if we put on some of that damned Christmas-tree mess they call 'lures,' we could catch something," Mr. Baines said as he raised the rod for another long cast, this one reaching down the shore ahead of them and dropping beside a fallen log. "But I don't call that fishing, do you? Stop the boat here for a minute while I work that log. Yes, some people would put on all that mess, sparkling and jiggling, about a half dozen hooks to snag the fish's belly at the same time the mouth is snagged, and call it fishing." He pulled in his line, raised the rod, let the line straighten out behind him, then again sent it down the lake to the log. "Yes, they call that fishing. The worst ones are those that do it at night with a flashlight. Savages." He pulled the bug back in tiny quick jerks, letting it float on the surface in between to tease any observing bass. "If they don't take that, they must not be here. All right, let's move along."

Leo looked over his shoulder and set his sights on the dock as they slowly approached the rock ledge that bulged out into the lake.

"You said your mother liked to fish," Mr. Baines commented. "Is she a bass fisherman?"

"Yes, sir. She likes to fly-rod for bass, the same as you do." Leo sure had to turn away now. His face must have been about ten shades of deep purple. He hadn't told such an all-out big lie in a long time—if ever. His mother liked to fish for bass, all right. But she nearly always used a lot of shiny, jiggly hooks, and sometimes at night!

"Is that so?" Mr. Baines said, cocking his head toward Leo. "You ought to get her in here one day, to fish with us. I bet she's pretty good."

Leo searched desperately for something to say that would get Mr. Baines onto another topic.

"Think she'd like to come in?" Mr. Baines asked.

"She works full-time, and then, when she has a day off, she has her special things she likes to do." He'd have to come up with something fast if Mr. Baines asked what they might be. "Oh! Look over there!" Leo cried out, taking a leaf from Mr. Baines's book.

"What is it?" The old man twisted his head about a quarter of the way around.

"Back across the lake," Leo quickly said.

"Damnation. Can't get my head turned that far around. What is it?"

"Something small and dark," he answered, looking at a stick floating by so he wouldn't be a total liar.

"Must be a beaver," Mr. Baines said, turning back

to look at his line lying idly in the water. "There are two families here. The beaver houses are down at the other end, on either side of the lake."

"Yes, sir." It had worked. George always was saying things like "Take a leaf from so-and-so's book" and "Turn the tables on him." One time he cheated a carpenter out of twenty-five dollars and said, "Just took a leaf from his own book; next time he won't charge me for a doorknob he got for free." That was just like George.

"Got one!" Mr. Baines stiffened at the same time his line went taut. "Doesn't feel like much of one, though. It'll probably be a little twelve-incher. Look at him, coming right in without any fight, like he wants to hop in the boat with us. There he is. Just reach down and release him, Leo. Let's let him grow up and learn some fight. And then we might as well row on over to the dock. I'm getting a mite thirsty." He glanced down at the thermos beside his foot. "Hope you remembered to put a stick in that iced tea."

"Yes, sir."

"You bring yourself a Coke?"

"Yes, sir. It's in our tackle bag."

Leo released the fish, washed his hands, and dried them on his pants legs, then repositioned the oars. "Straight across?"

"I think that's a good idea. I'll keep my eyes open for a rise, but I'm kind of running out of hope. This might be one of those mornings when we'd do better to just inspect lean-tos. I mean, we've got a job to do. Isn't that right?"

"Yes, sir," Leo agreed with him. Mr. Baines was having his iced tea pretty early, and that might mean a nap before lunch as well as after. Well, that was all right. Leo had plenty of thinking and figuring to do on his own.

Leo stood at the top of the rock ledge that rose twenty feet straight up from the lake and watched Mr. Baines slowly climb the path that sloped gently through the trees to the picnic site. The first few times they'd been here, he'd walked right behind the old man to make sure he got to the top all right—not that twenty feet was any big deal, but when you got to be eighty, it made it a little harder and higher.

But this time Leo had sprinted on ahead with the Coke and the thermos. He watched and waited and wondered how Mr. Baines made it at all with that heavy brace. Sometimes the old man would reach down and grab his pants leg and jerk it forward another inch before he put his weight on it. Then he'd step with the so-called good leg and position his body in a forward motion before he wrenched the other leg ahead. Once, early in the summer, Leo had offered to help him, but the stiffened fingers had motioned him away. After that, he pretended not to notice the facial grimaces or hear the grunts.

"All right, here I am." Mr. Baines waved his hand

jerkily at Leo and took the final step to the picnic table, where he sat heavily on the hard wooden bench. "That damned climb gets harder all the time. When I was a boy, we used to scamper right up that rock ledge." He bent his neck and chuckled. "We got plenty of spankings for ruining our pants, too."

Leo bet rich people didn't spank their kids the way poor people did. It wouldn't matter as much to them about the pants. They could just go out and buy more. Actually, he probably wouldn't get spanked either. But boy, would he ever get laid out! He'd be made to feel like a fool and a waster and a jerk who didn't care. A spanking would be a lot easier; it just happened and then it was over with.

The wind whispered through the tall pines around them and blew ripples across the water. Most of the songbirds had finished singing, their nesting seasons long since over, but occasional sweet notes filled the air. Leo had learned to recognize the melodies of the white-throated sparrow, which sang most of the summer, the scarlet tanager, and the rose-breasted grosbeak. He hadn't ever paid much attention to birds before this summer. But the people in here at the club were all bird-watchers, young and old alike, and even those who didn't seem to pay much attention, such as Pookie, even they knew one song from the other. It was just part of their store of knowledge. So Leo tried real hard to pay attention and to learn.

He looked up and watched a brown creeper walk

around the rough bark of a maple tree, half the time upside down as if it had no relation to gravity. And it reminded him of Creeper McGraw.

"Things look all right here," he commented.

Mr. Baines looked around. "Yes, no trash. The grill's beside the fireplace." He half turned on the bench. "Newspaper in the lean-to. See if the frying pan's been cleaned."

Leo checked. "It's all right. I'll see about the fire-wood." He stuck his head around the side of the lean-to. "Actually, it's pretty low. Enough for a few more fires, but not enough to last a whole week. Or I wouldn't think so."

Mr. Baines hauled himself to a standing position, and, stooped forward with his eyes on the ground, he hobbled to the side of the lean-to. "Well, you're right there. We'd better report this to Rastus. That's what we're here for. To let him know when we need something. Anything else?"

Leo checked the ax box, where the ax stayed, and the record book, where you wrote down the number of fish you caught, and the outhouse. The only thing that needed attention was the woodpile. He and Mr. Baines would stop by the superintendent's house and look for Rastus on the way back to the cottage. If they didn't find him then, they'd go back later on.

He again looked out over the lake, feeling the depth of privilege he was enjoying this summer. Everything was taken care of: boats, docks, wood, trails, cottages, even troughs for feeding the tame deer that strolled around the clearing. His mother would sure like to spend the summer in a place like this. It would be a treat for her, too.

Erastus Pike stood six-and-a-half feet tall and straight as a board. In summer, he wore his wool gray-flannel pants held up with red suspenders over a blue work shirt; in winter, he wore the same pants and suspenders over a heavy wool plaid shirt. He always wore a crumpled gray wide-brimmed hat on his head, no matter what the season was.

Leo had seen Rastus, as he was called by everyone, many times in town and at the hotel, where he frequently stopped by for a root beer. He had never been known to take anything else. George called him a "living legend." "Here comes the living legend," George would say, getting out a big heavy glass with a handle if he was behind the bar. Everyone local knew Rastus. It was said that he was the last of the old-time guides, and rumor had it that he had been raised by Indians. Leo would have believed anything. He stood in awe of the man and felt honored to be talking to him, and not just getting a nod when Rastus strode into the hotel.

"Now, Rastus," Mr. Baines said as he walked stiffly into the barn where Rastus was replacing the oarlocks on a rowboat, "Leo and I have been inspecting the lean-tos, and we notice the one at Split Rock is shy of wood." He paused beside the boat. "Another one of the colts got too rambunctious?"

Rastus turned his head to the side and spit a stream of brown tobacco juice out onto the dirt. "Yup."

Mr. Baines shook his head. "I don't remember that we broke so many oarlocks when we were young, but maybe I forget."

"Maybe they don't make 'em as good nowadays," Rastus replied. He noticed Leo and nodded his head in recognition.

"Maybe not. Maybe not," Mr. Baines said thoughtfully. "Well, we just wanted you to know about the wood."

"I'll tend to it."

"Leo here is a fine worker and helper," Mr. Baines said. "If you ever need an extra hand in the winter, he wouldn't disappoint you."

"I'll remember that, too," Rastus said, looking down the length of Leo.

Leo felt about six inches high. In spite of all the food he'd been packing in, he still was skinny and all sunk-in-looking. He wanted to say something important, but couldn't think of anything, and even if he had he wouldn't have been able to get it out.

"Catch anything?" Rastus asked Mr. Baines.

"Not a blessed thing worth talking about. We went around that far shore with a fine-toothed comb and found nothing."

"Must not be biting if you didn't catch one," Rastus said.

"That's what we decided. It wore me out, all that fruitless effort, and now I've got to go back and have a nap before lunch. Leo had a line out, too, quite a lot of the time, and he didn't even get a nibble. He's turning into a fine fisherman. He tells me his mother is a bass fisherman, and I said we ought to get her in here. Maybe she'd bring us some luck."

"She might."

"She likes to fly-rod for bass, same as we do. She knows what's fun."

Leo wanted to just sink into the ground and disappear. He felt his eyes stinging and clamped his teeth together. He stared at his feet.

"That so?" Rastus said in a slow drawl.

Leo could feel the living legend's eyes boring into him. He was beginning to feel sick to his stomach.

"Well, Leo, I guess we'd better move along. Miss Maudie said she wanted to go down the West Bay Trail without the dogs to see the family of otters, and this might be a good time for her. You could take care of those critters of hers while I take a little snooze. Be seeing you, Rastus." Mr. Baines limped back to the Jeep.

Leo was only too glad to get in the Jeep and hide behind the wheel. He hoped he never saw Rastus again the rest of the summer.

Leo had worried all through dinner about having been caught in such a stupid lie. Even if Rastus was the only one to know it so far, it wouldn't be long before Mr. Baines found out, and then there'd be Miss Maudie and Tigger and Pookie and Creeper McGraw and everyone else. Leo was a plain out-and-out liar. And the reason he'd lied was to pretend he came from better people than he did.

He felt so rotten he'd barely eaten any pot roast and only had one piece of lemon-meringue pie. Even Miss Maudie commented on his lack of appetite and worried that he might be coming down with a cold.

Now Leo sat up in his room on the end of the bed and couldn't remember when he'd felt so dejected. If George were here, he'd say Leo had the potential of sinking into a real depression.

Leo got up and walked over to the window and looked out at the small yellowish lights sprinkled across the slope of the clearing. That one, way up the hill, would be from the cottage where Beek and Tigger and some others were playing Trivial Pursuit or poker. That one, closer by, was where this week's tennis champion lived. And way up, beyond most of the cottages, up by the darkened barn silhouetted against the pale sky, was Rastus's house. He'd probably be watching television. He was the only one to have a set. Mr. Baines had said most people didn't miss it one bit, that they came here to get away from that sort of thing.

Leo didn't want to be ashamed of his mother, but he was. He was ashamed of the way she looked and the way she acted and the way she didn't know how to do the proper things. The members of the club were fine people. They were born with the kind of advantages that made it easy for them to distinguish between fly fishing and Christmas-tree fishing, between reading books and watching game shows on TV, between being a real family unit and living with your boyfriend.

Even if Tigger and Pookie never saw their father and rarely their mother, they were a family unit with their grandfather and great-aunt, and that counted just as much. It was dignified. The way Leo and his mother lived wasn't. It was as simple as that.

Leo could hear Mr. Baines clumping around downstairs. It would soon be time for him to go to bed.

"Leo?"

"Yes, sir!" Leo quickly opened his door and went to the top of the stairs. "You ready to come up?" He started down, peering over the banister, seeing Nectarine chase Louisa across the rug, snapping at her tail, while Tossie waited near Miss Maudie's feet.

"Leo," Mr. Baines said, "I'm not a bit sleepy yet, and Miss Maudie thought you might like to learn how to play bridge. What do you think of that? Or are you not feeling up to it?"

"Oh, I feel fine. But don't we need four people to play bridge?"

"We have four," the old man answered. "Pookie's here tonight. Guess she didn't want to play poker with the crowd."

"Pookie's here? Here in the house?"

"Right out on the porch, getting a little night air."

Leo took this in. On the one night he had a chance to go to the lake alone, Mr. Baines, after two naps, was wide awake. "Well, don't you want to play with your regular people?" he asked Miss Maudie.

"Can't. Mrs. McAllister has a toothache again tonight. Stop that running around in here! I should have taken them with me on that walk today. They haven't used up their energy. Sit down!"

Mr. Baines tucked his head down into his chest and chuckled. "A lot of good it'll do to tell them anything."

Miss Maudie leaned forward on the sofa. "Good girl, Tossie. You just stay put." She patted the brown-and-white head. "Well, you want to learn, Leo?"

"Oh, sure. I sure do." Bridge. Wow. He hoped it didn't take too much concentration. He was low on that tonight.

"Good." Mr. Baines slapped his skinny thigh. "How about running and getting Pookie."

Leo went out the back hallway door, near the kitchen, and circled the house before he found Pookie tucked into a big slat-backed Adirondack chair, with her spine curved into an almost impossible bend and her cheek resting on her knees.

"There you are," he said, stopping in front of her. "Your grandfather wants to know if you want to play bridge."

She slowly raised her head. "Bridge?"

"Yeah, you know. Bridge. I don't know how, but Miss Maudie says she'll teach me."

"She taught me."

"Yeah, well, I guess. You want to play?"

"Am I supposed to come in?"

Leo looked around at the darkened porch, with no visible signs of a light. "Uh, yeah," he said. "Inside."

"Who's playing?"

"Miss Maudie and Mr. Baines." Leo found himself leaning over her chair and lowering his voice. "Mr.

Baines sent me out to get you."

"Oh." Pookie gave her head a quick little shake. "Grandpa wants me?"

"Yeah."

"Oh, yes. I'm coming." She tipped one foot over the front of the chair and let it touch the floor. Then the other one followed. She leaned forward, and her body rose the way mist rises off the lake on a cold morning.

Leo stepped back and watched. She was ghostly, in her long white shirt and too-short underwear. "You want to play?" he asked.

"Sure," she replied, sliding past him toward the door near the middle of the porch. "Sure. You want to play?"

"Oh, yeah, I'm coming." He followed her, with a sadness swelling up inside him. She needed someone, but he didn't know who it was.

Leo understood about the suits and about trumps. But when Miss Maudie got into bidding, he had no idea what she was talking about. He had only half paid attention, figuring he'd catch on as they played. Now he knew he was in big trouble. This was a game that required concentration, and his was "out to lunch."

George said that, the time Leo was supposed to be taking inventory of the cleaning supplies in the storage room at the hotel. "All he had to do was count the Drāno cans and write it down, and he got it wrong.

How much Drāno can we have? His concentration is right out to lunch. I know the boy can count, because I saw that *A* on his math paper. If they have a course in concentration, be sure and sign him up." George had said that to Leo's mother, but he'd waited until the bar was about half full, and then there'd been a big laugh up and down the stools.

"Now, Leo, you think you understand?" Miss Maudie asked.

He swallowed hard. "I hope so."

Pookie turned her head to him and smiled. "Don't worry. Miss Maudie's so good, she can play for the both of you. Grandpa plays for me."

Leo and Miss Maudie were paired against Pookie and Mr. Baines. Leo figured they were about even. Pookie might know how to play, but she was having trouble seeing the spots on the cards. Leo could see fine, but he suddenly couldn't remember whether a six was higher than a seven or vice-versa. This was going to be a night to remember.

The play started, and it took Leo so long to say anything when it got to be his turn to bid that Miss Maudie finally announced she was going to help him. She stood up, marched around to his chair, and inspected his hand. Then she told him what to do and returned to her seat.

Pookie and Mr. Baines went on just as if nothing out of the ordinary had happened. When it came around to Leo again, he just looked across the table at Miss Maudie and waited for her to tell him what to do.

So they managed to get through the first hand pretty well. With unbelievable good luck, Leo was the dummy on the next and sat back in his chair just watching the others.

Miss Maudie told him what to do again on the third hand, and the rest of the game went by smoothly. Leo felt like a permanent dummy, but at least he didn't make a fool of himself by saying the wrong thing.

"Does Tigger play?" he asked Pookie.

"Oh, sure," she said. "We all do."

The dogs started to get restless after about an hour into the bridge game, and occasionally Miss Maudie had to yell at them to sit down so she could concentrate. Two times they knocked over a small table near the door and sent the ashtray, car keys, and box of pencils sailing across the rug. Leo had to keep jumping up to retrieve things. The third time they did it, Mr. Baines decided to take action. He hobbled across the room and picked up the things himself. He put the pencils and ashtray on another table; then he put the keys in his jacket pocket.

"Think I ought to move the table?" he asked, peering over his glasses at Miss Maudie.

"Of course not," she snapped. "They're not going to bother it."

He raised his eyebrows in a skeptical gesture at Leo

and Pookie; then he hobbled back to his chair, a low chuckle rumbling up from his chest. "Of course not," he said, still chuckling. "They never bother anything. They never bump into things or knock things over or make any fuss at all."

"It's your play," Miss Maudie said, setting her lips in a thin line. "But maybe you'd rather grumble about incidentals."

"No," he said, shaking his head in an innocent manner. "I don't want to grumble about anything. I never have liked to grumble." He looked at Pookie and winked.

Pookie smiled at him. "Oh, Grandpa," she said, "your kind of grumbling is nice."

"There, you see," Miss Maudie commented in a rather superior way, "even Pookie notices your grumbling. Sit down! I can't think! Sit!"

"If you can't think, it may be our superior playing has upset you," Mr. Baines said.

"Hmmmph!" Miss Maudie snorted. "Superior playing, indeed. Leo is a born learner. He's caught right on and"—she craned her neck to look at the score pad—"I believe we're ahead." She paused and looked at Leo. "You've played very well. Not that you haven't, Pookie. But I'm afraid you've had the disadvantage of Grandpa nodding off a bit."

"Nodding off," Mr. Baines repeated in a slow gravelly kind of voice. "Nodding off, indeed." He dipped his chin to his chest and chuckled, his shoulders jerking up and down. "The only thing wrong with this game is the interruptions we've had from the peanut gallery." He raised his eyes and stared at the dogs, now lying on the long sofa. "I'm glad they've made themselves comfortable," he added in a soft, sarcastic voice. "And speaking of nodding off, Leo and I have to get up early and make a trip to Thumb Pond to catch the early rise. Want to have a quick go at it before breakfast, Leo?"

"Before breakfast?" Miss Maudie interrupted. "What makes you think you can get up so early?"

"I can get up if it means catching the early rise. What do you say, Leo?"

"Yes, sir. Sounds fine to me."

"Good. Wonder if Tigger would like to come."

"He'll be out late," Miss Maudie answered. "I expect he'll sleep through the early rise."

"And how do you know he'll be out late?" Mr. Baines asked.

"I heard him tell Beek at dinner he would play Trivial Pursuit with her alone, and you know how long that will take. I think it was a sort of challenge."

"Well, I guess that does let him out. Then Leo and I will bring back the fish for lunch alone. Won't we, Leo?"

"Yes, sir."

"Well, this hand's over. We might as well stop here," Miss Maudie said.

Miss Maudie took the dogs outside while Leo and Mr. Baines went through their nightly routine. When everyone, the dogs included, was in his or her room, with the doors shut, Leo put on his trunks, got dressed again, and sat on the side of the bed to wait for the snoring to start. This was the one night he was sure Pookie wouldn't be down at the lake, and he was determined to get on with his swimming. He shivered just thinking about the cold air and water. But his mind was made up.

Mr. Baines began his rhythmic rumbling, which was more like roaring in the stillness of the house, and Leo tiptoed out of his room and down the stairs. He wasn't too worried about the dogs. If one of them heard the floor creak and began barking, Miss Maudie would probably just yell for quiet. And Pookie was bound to be off somewhere in her own world. All in all, Leo felt pretty safe.

A light by the sofa had been left on for Tigger, but the rest of the big room was in deep shadows. Leo paused at the bottom of the stairs. Weird shapes spread up the walls. The antlers of the deer heads slid upward at a distorted angle and disappeared into darkness. The furniture seemed low and hunched between the blackened windows.

Leo could feel his heart quickening, and his hand felt cold on the newel post at the end of the banister. He almost wished Pookie were at the lake instead of upstairs so he would be forced to stay in his bed.

He stepped quietly onto the carpet and directed his feet toward the darkened back hall. As he passed the end of the big table beneath the stairs, he got a prickly feeling at the base of his neck. It was as if he sensed someone else in the room. He stopped and slowly turned his head. The room was empty. He took a deep breath and moved slowly forward, his heart racing. He knew it was silly of him. There was no one. Still, he had an uncanny insight that he was not alone. He forced himself to step into the blackened hallway. And just as he did, a hand reached out and touched his arm.

Leo almost fainted. He jumped so high he actually had to grab his chest to keep himself from screaming. "Who is it?" he gasped.

"Shut up!" a voice commanded. "Don't wake anybody up."

Tigger. "Oh, wow! You scared me." Leo heard his voice tremble. "What are you doing here?"

"I'm looking for the station-wagon keys. They're always on that little table. But I can't find them." Tigger pointed to the table the dogs had knocked against. "Have you seen them?"

Leo cleared his throat. He wanted his voice to come out normal. "Mr. Baines has them. He picked them up off the floor and put them in his pocket."

"Damn! I need them."

Leo wondered why. He knew that Tigger used the

station wagon only for going to Mink to swim or for an errand around the clearing, and only then when Mr. Baines had the Jeep.

"That Jeep makes so much noise, I'll wake up the whole clearing." Tigger muttered this as if it explained everything.

"Oh," Leo said. He looked longingly toward the front door, but Tigger stayed right where he was.

"I want to go to town," Tigger said finally.

"You want to go to town *now*?" Leo thought he must have misunderstood.

"Yes, I've got a date there."

Leo looked around the darkened room. "You taking Beek?"

"Beek? Don't be a fool. Of course I'm not taking Beek. I'm meeting one of the waitresses from the dining room out near the end of the road. Listen, Leo, I need your help. You wouldn't want me to stand her up, would you? No, that's right, you wouldn't. Think you could help me get the car keys?"

"I don't know." Leo forgot all about Mink Pond.

"Come on," Tigger urged. "You know where Grandpa keeps his jacket. Just sneak in and get the keys out of the pocket."

Leo couldn't believe his ears. "You mean, steal them?"

"If you want to call it that. Then you can slip them back tomorrow morning when Grandpa goes to the bathroom. He'll never know. What do you say?"

"I don't think so . . ."

"You're the only one who can do it. You want to help me, don't you?"

"Sure, but . . ." Leo tried to think of a good reason he couldn't do it.

"Come on, Leo. Be a sport. I can't have her out there waiting for me. Something might happen to her." Tigger looked down at Leo and waited.

Leo backed into the living room and glanced up the stairs. The snoring was still going strong in its deep-sleep pattern. "Well, maybe . . ."

"Good. You're a real friend. I'll wait here. If Miss Maudie gets up or Pookie stirs around or anything, I'll give you some kind of signal. Now get going."

Leo crept back up the stairs, one silent heavy step at a time. With each upward thrust of his body, he felt himself sinking inward, and the pounding in his chest got heavier. He wasn't really going to steal anything. But he was about to betray the old man's trust in him. He knew he was about to do something wrong, but he kept moving forward like a mechanical toy that has no control of itself.

Leo went through his bedroom and quietly opened the connecting door to Mr. Baines's room. The snoring surged at him, like the voice of a supernatural being urging him on. He stared at the open mouth and closed eyes, clearly visible in the moonlit room. The gnarled hands were limply draped across the fold of the blanket.

What if those old eyes suddenly opened and fixed him with their watery stare? What would he do? How could he lie his way out of this? He quickly dropped to his knees and crawled across the floor, his eyes on the jacket hanging over the back of a straight chair. Silvery spears of light traced the heavy brace lying beside the chair leg. Leo's heart pounded. Its icy glare made him afraid to touch it. He cautiously reached across and touched the jacket, holding his breath, waiting for the next gargled intake of air from the bed. His hand slid to the pocket and he felt inside, his fingers touching the cold keys. Slowly he withdrew his hand, clutching the keys tightly to keep them from jiggling. He turned in a slow circle and crawled back out of the room.

In his own room, Leo, still on his hands and knees, reached up and pushed the door shut. Then he sat sideways and felt the keys. He was guilty now. Even if he took them right back and lied to Tigger, he was still guilty. He had done something wrong and he knew it, even if no one else ever found out.

He stood up and walked out of the room and down the stairs. "Here," he said to Tigger, handing him the keys.

"Thanks, thanks a lot." Tigger zipped up his heavy hooded sweatshirt and folded the keys in the palm of his hand. "I'll do the same for you someday." And with that he turned and went silently down the hall and out the door.

Leo heard the faint muffled drone of the car engine. He wondered how many nights Tigger had driven to town, starting the station wagon without waking anyone, even the dogs. Maybe it happened so often it got to be one of those subconscious sounds that don't mean anything.

Leo sat down on the bottom step, biting his lower lip until it hurt. He felt very small and lowly and miserable.

Leo had never spent such a restless night. It was worse than the times he used to wait by the door until his mother came home from the hotel.

For a long time he sat in the darkened living room waiting for Tigger to return. As the hours went by, he grew more and more sick at heart. Finally he went upstairs and stretched out on his bed, staring at the silvery moonlight on the ceiling. He tried to convince himself it was nothing, that Tigger wouldn't do anything really wrong. This was just some harmless stuff, nothing to sweat over. But every time he got to thinking in that direction and trying to feel better, there'd be a big flip-flop in his mind and he'd be overwhelmed by the sneakiness of his act.

Leo fretted and twisted, bringing the pillow up on

the sides of his head and pressing it against his ears. He dreaded the morning, when he would have to get the keys back into Mr. Baines's jacket. It was possible that Tigger would forget and leave them in the car, and how would Leo explain their whereabouts to Mr. Baines then? Finally, exhausted with worry and shame, Leo sank into a fitful sleep.

He woke with a start when he heard Mr. Baines coughing. Pale gray light filled the window. It was morning! Leo sat up with a start. He heard Mr. Baines limping down the hall toward the bathroom, and Leo automatically turned his head in the direction of the door.

There! There, on the floor inside his room were the keys! He jumped out of bed and grabbed them, then ran to the connecting door. He carefully opened it and peered into the room. The rumpled bed was empty. The room was empty. With a racing heart, Leo rushed to the chair and put the keys back in the jacket pocket. Then he quickly returned to his room and breathed deep heaves of relief. It was done, and no one the wiser—except himself.

Soon Mr. Baines tapped on his door. "Leo? You awake?"

"Yes, sir."

"Want to catch the early rise?"

"Yes, sir."

"Well, shake a leg. I slept like a baby and am full of

energy. Hope you feel the same way."

"Yes, sir, I sure do." Leo opened his door and tried to smile at Mr. Baines, hoping he would last through lunch.

Somehow Leo made it through the morning. He managed to drive the Jeep to Thumb Pond and then row Mr. Baines around the shore twice. Two times around! And it was a pretty big lake. They stopped at the island to check the lean-to, the fireplace, the wood supply, and the condition of the outhouse. Satisfied, they returned to the boat and continued their slow pursuit of the wary brook trout that lived in the cool depths of the water, nearing the shore in the early morning before the sun warmed the surface.

By the time they returned to the dock, they had two plump trout in the net and had released six more.

"Well, that wasn't a bad morning's catch, was it?" Mr. Baines asked as he leaned on an oar and watched Leo tie the boat to a giant screw eye on the side of the dock.

"No, sir, it sure wasn't." Leo's back ached, and he turned away from the old man to hide the frown on his face. He just wanted to go back to bed.

"We've got some pretty good reports to turn in to Creeper when we get to the annual meeting. Maybe we'll give them to him ahead of time and let him report. On the other hand, it's customary for committee chairmen to give their own reports at this big meeting. At the little one, in July, they mostly talk about new members and any new rules that might apply for the summer. But this is the big business meeting. Yes, we'll do it that way. You'll have to go with me to make sure I don't forget anything. It's Labor Day weekend, and you'll still be here. Look over there!"

Leo didn't even bother to look. He just went on picking up their gear and making sure they didn't leave anything behind. It would be just about unforgivable for the chairman to leave a mess.

Mr. Baines looked at his watch. "We have time to get to the dining room before they shut the doors. There's nothing like getting up with the birds and taking a turn on the lake before breakfast. That hot cereal will taste pretty good this morning. Pretty good."

In the afternoons, if they weren't fishing, Leo was put in charge of the dogs while Miss Maudie took her "constitutional." That's what she called going for a walk. After the hottest part of the day had passed and before it was time to get ready for dinner, she walked around the clearing, usually all the way past the barn and Rastus's house and onto the pasture, where the sky opened up and the distant mountains rose mysteriously with no visible connection to the earth.

Tossie was being a pain, as she usually was when Miss Maudie left her, whining and whimpering and pacing to the door and back. Nectarine and Louisa would stop goofing around when they heard the pathetic sounds and would whine a little themselves. But they resumed their playing when Tossie shut up and started pacing. They were chasing each other around the house, snarling and snapping—first Nectarine hot on Louisa's tail, then they reversed. If Nectarine stopped to scratch, Louisa raced into the kitchen and threw her front paws up on the little table beneath the window and looked for Miss Maudie. She'd pant, wagging her tail like a white flag flapping in a strong wind, then rush back out.

Leo didn't dare yell at them too much, for fear Miss Maudie might suddenly return. He just braced himself when they shot past and hoped they wouldn't break anything while he was in charge.

Mr. Baines had decided to visit someone two cottages away. Leo offered to drive him there, but he insisted he could walk by himself. Leo watched through the kitchen window as the old man, hunched and dragging one leg, propelled himself forward by swinging his arms and shoulders in a kind of churning motion. Finally he got to his destination. Leo breathed a sigh of relief and took some molasses cookies out of the big jar and began to nibble on one.

There was sure one thing you could say for the older generation, he reflected: they didn't waver in their beliefs, and they never pretended to be something they weren't. But with the younger ones—it was hard to tell.

Take Pookie. If you just met her casually, you'd think she was some kind of freak, with her too-short long underwear and men's shirts and that faraway look. But underneath, she just needed someone to take care of her, like a forgotten doll that was outgrown and left in the bottom of a closet. Leo knew that feeling. It was one he could understand. There were plenty of times he watched his mother and George laughing and whispering, their arms around each other's waists, having forgotten Leo was in the room, maybe even forgotten he was in the world.

And Tigger—about as straight-arrow as anyone you ever saw, and it turns out he's got this secret night life, sneaking out to date the local girls when he's supposed to be practically engaged to Beek.

Leo felt a big emptiness way down inside him. It was more than the shame he felt for having been sneaky with Mr. Baines. It was hard to explain, even to himself. Maybe it was because he didn't understand the ways of these people and probably never would. Maybe it was because he was different, as his mother had said. For him, town meant home. But Tigger seemed to think it was some low-down spot that wasn't good enough for his real friends. Leo had wanted to believe that if he drove a Jeep and wore cut-off blue jeans and knew how to fly-fish and play bridge, he would be superior, the way Tigger was. But now he wasn't sure. Maybe you had to be born to this life to understand it. Maybe it was hopeless for him to dream of improving himself.

That was it. He had lost the incentive of his dream. George would love to get hold of that. "Incentive" was one of his favorite words: "I had the incentive to improve myself when I was a boy, and I did. It was just a matter of time before I got my hands on running this hotel. Now, Leo here seems to lack incentive. I know an ordinary carrot on a stick wouldn't incite much interest, and it's doubtful a whole carrot farm would do the trick. Of course, I hadn't considered putting a hamburger on a stick, but maybe that would do it." And everyone at the bar had laughed and looked at Leo, the way they always did.

George always made these remarks when there were umpteen people at the bar. Come to think of it, the bar was full most of the time. George was real popular. He didn't care whether you bought a drink or not. He'd let people sit on a bar stool all day, without a glass of anything in front of them, just talking and being friendly.

128

Incentive. Maybe George was right. If Leo could hang on to his dream of a better life, he might still make it happen. He sure wasn't ready to give up yet.

He ate another molasses cooky, crunching it between his back teeth and letting the melted sugar trickle down his throat. If he could get out of the house tonight without interruption, he'd go to Mink Pond and make himself swim out as far as he could. He just needed practice. And even if it didn't make him a high-class person, at least he would be able to swim with his classmates when they went on the Polliwog Picnic next spring.

"Hi. How's it going?"

Startled, Leo turned to see Tigger walking into the room. "Hi." Tigger didn't look any worse for having indulged in his sneaky life.

"Grandpa still sleeping?"

"No, he's gone visiting."

"You going fishing when he gets back?"

"Don't know. I suppose, if there's time before dinner."

Tigger reached past him into the cooky jar. "I thought I'd run up to the High Beaver Dam and see if the little buggers have added another foot to it. You been up there?"

Leo nodded. "Mr. Baines and I drove up last week to look at it. The beavers were swimming around in the water."

Tigger chewed thoughtfully. "Want to come with me?"

Leo looked away, out the window where the long shadows from the larch trees were stretching across the road and dried clearing grasses toward the east. "I guess not. I'll wait for Mr. Baines."

"You don't sound very happy about it."

"It's nothing to do with Mr. Baines that's made me unhappy," Leo said.

"You mean you're mad at me," Tigger said matter-of-factly.

"Yeah, that's part of it. I'm mad at myself, too. Maybe mostly that."

"You didn't do anything wrong, and neither did I. There's no harm in having a date in town."

"Then how come you won't take Beek out there?"

Tigger shrugged. "I don't take Beek because I like seeing someone else every now and again. Beek and I have been thrown together since we were in diapers. Maybe I like her enough to call her a special friend, but that doesn't mean I have to spend every spare minute with her. She understands. We're good friends, but I see other girls and she sees other boys."

"I thought Mr. Baines said you and she were . . ." Leo couldn't find the right words.

"Oh, I know what Grandpa says. But that's wishful thinking. Beek and I are real good friends, and that's all there is to it."

130

"But the waitress . . ." Again, Leo was tongue-tied and didn't know how to finish.

"What about her? She's pretty, we had a date. That's all there is to it."

"I thought you meant town wasn't good enough for Beek, but it was for a waitress."

"That's dumb. Town's plenty good enough for Beek or anyone else. It's good enough for you and your family, isn't it?"

"Sure it is." Leo fumbled his hand around in the cooky jar and pulled out a broken corner. He held it in the palm of his hand. "You still shouldn't have asked me to get the keys for you."

"Come on, Leo. You were the logical one. You knew where they were. You're making a mountain out of a molehill. It was all a very innocent occurrence."

"Then why don't you tell Mr. Baines about it?"

Tigger stared at him a long moment; then he said, "You win. It wasn't the right thing to do. If I had wanted a date out in town, I should have said so in front of everyone. I did go behind their backs." He paused. "Sorry I involved you."

"That's okay. It doesn't matter." He put the broken cooky in his mouth and reached for another.

"You seen Pookie?" Tigger finally asked.

"No." And why don't you do something to help her? Leo wanted to ask. No one cared about anyone else except themselves. Tigger didn't care if he got Leo in trouble, as long as he got the car keys he needed; he didn't care what happened to Pookie, as long as he didn't have to do more than row her around and see that she got to meals on time. "What's wrong with her anyway?"

Tigger looked out the window. "She's just at loose ends. It's not that big a deal. At least up here she keeps out of trouble and doesn't get in with a bad crowd and get hurt. She'll straighten out when she wants to."

"Think she can?"

"Sure." He opened the refrigerator door and took out a Coke. "As soon as she has some reason to."

Leo wondered how big a reason that would have to be. "What do Miss Maudie and Mr. Baines think about her?"

Tigger turned and looked at Leo for the first time. "Grandpa only sees that she's a lonely little girl. Miss Maudie sees more than that, but doesn't know what to do about it. But they care about her and she knows it. That's a lot."

"Yeah, I guess it is." Leo could see that Tigger really cared about Pookie. But Tigger sure was underestimating Mr. Baines. Mr. Baines might be old and decrepit and drink a bit too much Scotch, but he didn't miss much. And Leo bet he knew more than Tigger ever would. Mr. Baines never would have asked Leo to do something dishonest.

Tigger snapped open the Coke and took a swallow. "I'll go find her and take her with me. If Grandpa wants the Jeep, tell him where I've gone, okay?"

Before Leo could answer, a small voice spoke from the doorway, "Where are you going?"

Leo and Tigger both turned to see Pookie inside the kitchen. She had arrived as silently as the summer air trapped in the big house. She stood limply, her shoulders rounded, her mouth open and her teeth together. She frowned at them, as if she were concentrating to be able to see them across the room. "What are you doing?" she whispered.

Judging by the way she looked, Leo thought it was a miracle she could stand or speak at all. "Pookie . . ." he began.

Tigger quickly stepped forward and put his free hand on her arm. "Come on," he said. He set the Coke on the counter and steered Pookie out of the room and into the back hallway.

Leo listened to the back door clicking shut, the muffled footsteps on the wooden porch, finally the Jeep doors banging to and the motor being revved up. He turned and watched the gravel kicking up from the spinning tires and the Jeep tearing up the road in a cloud of dust. Tigger had gotten her away before the Baineses came home.

Leo stared at the empty road for a long time, then turned and started across the room just as the dogs came streaking into the back hall, barking and jumping up and down.

He went back and looked out the window at the

sounds of the familiar voices. There came the old people strolling down memory lane, probably talking about how the road used to be fifty years ago. When they neared, he heard them.

"We never had black flies like this when we were children," Mr. Baines said, waving his hand around his head.

"Of course we did," Miss Maudie snapped. "They have always been around. You just walk slower now and let them catch up with you. Oh, Leo! Let the dogs out, will you?" She motioned at the window with the little basket she always carried. Leo wondered if she had picked wild blueberries. He opened the back door, and the dogs tumbled out while the two old people moved slowly into the house.

L eo stepped into the water that lay darkly beneath the canoe dock. The moon had taken on a lopsided shape, but still it spread its light across the flat surface of the lake, bathing the distant shore in an eerie glow. The air settled on his shoulders in an icy pall, and he folded his arms across his chest.

He waded gingerly out, still hugging himself, until the water reached his waist. Then he realized that the water felt warmer than the air. Taking a deep breath and throwing his arms out wide, he suddenly ducked beneath the surface, head and all, almost sitting on the sandy bottom covered with a thick layer of slick mud.

Coming up quickly, he shook his head, flinging water in quick half circles from his hair, and let out his breath. "Wow!" he exclaimed softly. He was really in it. He was about to meet his challenge. He was about to conquer his childishness and swim.

He stayed close to the end of the dock, going back

and forth, trying to make his head go down and his back come up. He mastered the arm strokes, pulling back with his elbow and cupping his fingers the way he had seen good swimmers do when they reached forward. First one arm, then the other. Over and over. But he couldn't get his legs to coordinate with his arms. His legs stuck out at sideways angles from his body and kicked bent-kneed, the way a frog does when it glides on the surface.

He finally held on to the end of the dock and practiced extending his legs straight behind him, kicking up and down. He held on with the tips of his fingers and lowered his face into the water. He turned his head to the side to take a breath of air, then lowered it and blew out his breath in a bubbly rush when his face was submerged.

Leo repeated all the separate parts of the art of swimming until he had them pretty well understood. Now all he had to do was to put it all together.

What the heck, he thought. If he pushed away from the dock and pretended he was still holding on, he could get a better feel of his progress.

Floating face down, Leo let go of the dock and kicked his legs up and down. It felt okay. Next he extended his arms and turned his head to take a breath. So far, so good. Then he pulled his elbow back and got ready to extend his arm while he was kicking.

By really concentrating, he was able to get his arms

and legs to work together. He knew he hadn't moved very far in the water, but that was unimportant at the moment. Kick, reach, breathe. There it was. He was actually doing it. Kick, reach, breathe. One leg, then the other. One arm, then the other. The breathing was the hardest to remember. He had to force himself to turn his head, and then he was practically bursting his lungs before he could do it. But he did, and that was the main thing.

He didn't know how long he had been practicing when he paused, going vertical and doing the leg paddle as he looked around. Dark shadows had taken the place of the dock and the rows of canoes. In the other direction lay nothing but the glassy moonlit expanse. His heart skipped a beat. Water and shadows were all he could see. He had no idea how far he was from the shadows, or even what they were. When he blinked real hard and cleared his eyes, they seemed miles away. When he squinted, the dark looming objects appeared to be unreal with no connection to the shore at all.

Leo knew he was beginning to panic. He could feel it rising up in him from the pit of his stomach, through his tight chest, and into his throat. He wanted to cry out, but he was still enough in control to keep himself from doing that.

"No," he said out loud. "No, don't panic. Stop and think."

His mind flashed to George. What would George do if he were in this fix?

He wheeled around again and stared into the distance. George would assess the situation and make a calm judgment. George would pick out the shadow that seemed the strongest and then swim toward it. Never mind if he was at some strange part of the shoreline when he got to it. He could always walk back to the dock, even if he had to walk all the way around the lake to get there.

Leo took some deep breaths. His eyes set on an object that appeared to be the closest to him. If he kept his eye on it, he wouldn't end up going around in circles.

He thrust outward in the water, not lowering his head but staring with open eyes ahead of him. His arms splashed as he tried to bring them forward in an expert manner. His legs kept sinking downward and going bent-kneed. He thrashed ahead, terrified. Could he make it?

As he struggled, he gasped. His breath came in quick jerks, and he could feel tears stinging his eyes. The dark shore was as distant as ever. Maybe he was going in circles anyway. No, he told himself desperately, he had to be going straight. He just had to be. He gasped again and felt the water suck into his lungs.

His face went under, and he fought to get his head up again. His arms desperately reached upward as he gave some mighty kicks with his legs. With his head above the water, he coughed, looking upward as his mouth opened, trying to catch his breath and clear it.

"Help!" he cried involuntarily.

With that, a thin white arm reached out and touched his shoulder.

"It's all right! I've got you!"

"Pookie!" Leo gasped, and sank under, tangled in billowing white cloth that wound around his head.

The four arms clutched at each other as they slowly went down toward the bottom of the lake. Leo struggled to get the shirt away from his head, and when he did, it was too black to see the figure holding on to him. But he could feel the grip on his arm and knew Pookie was trying to hold him. He also knew in a flash that she was too frail to be able to do it and that they both would drown.

Downward they spiraled, Pookie but a pale blur in front of him. Leo could feel the shirt folding itself around them both as it floated upward and outward. He fought to push her away, but she clung to him. Her body slid next to him, and she wrapped her arms around him. Leo grabbed at the shirt, but could no longer feel it. The water began to slide away from him, and he dropped motionlessly in a black void with no feeling.

But then his feet touched the thick slime at the bottom of the lake. Leo reacted quickly and thrust with all his might, scissoring his legs, one arm clutching Pookie and the other fighting the water above them. Still

Pookie held on to him, and he could feel her legs kicking next to his.

And the next thing Leo knew was when they burst through the water and into the black night air.

They both gasped and struggled on the surface. And then they were leaning in the same direction, and their arms were moving and their legs were kicking.

Before Leo knew it, his feet again touched bottom, but this time his head was in the air. Clinging to each other, he and Pookie dragged themselves out onto the bank. They dropped in the wet sand at the water's edge and coughed, retching and gasping, until they got their breaths.

Leo realized he would be dead at the bottom of the lake if it hadn't been for Pookie. She had somehow heard him and had come to his rescue.

"Oh, Highpockets," Pookie said softly. "How can I ever thank you? I went out there to help you and just ended up almost drowning us both."

"You did?"

"Oh, yes. I was such a fool to hang on to your neck. I should have just held your arm."

"But I was the one who pulled you down," Leo said.

"No, you weren't. You saved me from sinking into that mud and dying."

Leo shook his head and looked out over the lake. "How far out were we?"

"Far enough," she answered.

Leo could see Pookie's small thin shoulders shaking. "You're freezing."

"Yes," she whispered, the chattering of her teeth as loud as her voice. "You must be, too."

"No," he lied, "I don't have on a wet shirt. Where are we?"

"The boat house is just over there," she answered, pointing with her right arm.

"Oh, yeah, I see it. I've got some dry clothes by the canoes. Come on. You can have my jacket."

Leo moved to help Pookie to her feet, but she got up on her own. They sloshed along the shore to the canoe dock. There they climbed up the bank.

"Here," Leo said, handing her the jacket. "It's got a lining and will help some."

Pookie turned her back to him and pulled the wet shirt over her head. She put on the jacket and zipped it up. "Oh, that feels good," she said.

Leo got his shirt on. "I never saw you before I went in the water."

"I got here as you were practicing. You're good, you know."

"No, I'm not."

"Yes, you are. You've got a good strong arm stroke and your kick is good. All you need to do is go out more and get used to it."

Leo looked at her. She sounded as if she knew what she was talking about. Mr. Baines had bragged about her swimming so much, too, but Leo had figured she was too stoned all the time to be able to do it. But her instincts must have just propelled her into the water and out to him when she saw he needed help. Yeah, she must be good. Swimming was as natural to her as walking. Pookie the seal, Mr. Baines had called her. "I'd like to get better. I feel like I could do it, too."

"Sure you could. Swimming's a lot of fun."

"How come you never do it, then?"

She ducked her head. "I used to."

"Why don't you now?"

"I don't know. I just don't think about it."

Leo looked away from her. Her voice was so strong. The water and the exertion, to say nothing of the panic, must have sobered her up. She had just proved she could pull herself together in short order if she had to, just as Tigger had said. Someone ought to tell her to do it on a permanent basis. Someone ought to talk to her and tell her she was wasting her life. You'd think her own family would care enough to at least give it a try.

"We ought to go back," Pookie said quietly. Her hand fluttered and she reached for her wet shirt. She stuck her fingers into the pocket of the shirt and pulled out a small soaking-wet package. She held it in her hand and stared at it. "They're all wet and ruined," she said sadly. "That's all right. There's more at the house."

"Pookie," Leo began, then hesitated. He looked at her and the wet bundle in her small hand. "How come you want that junk? It just messes up your head. Oh, I know you told me it makes you forget. But you ought to remember. There's so much that's nice, and you ought to remember it. Right now, you could remember that you saved me from drowning."

"But I didn't."

"Yes, you did. I'd be dead if it weren't for you. Your mind's not so messed up it can't understand that. Please, Pookie. Don't smoke that junk. Stay off it and go swimming with me."

She put the wet package back into the shirt pocket. "It doesn't matter. No one cares what I do."

"That's not true. I care." And he did. He cared as much as the others. If he didn't speak up, he would be just as much to blame as they were. "I care. You're pretty. You're nice. You're a good swimmer. You can do all those things like play cards and games and the other things that go on around here at night. You could be doing those things and having a good time. Look what you're missing."

"You miss it," she said softly and turned her head to look at him.

"I miss it because I have to. I'm not included. But you're different. You're included in everything—or would be if you wanted to be. You have everything and you're wasting it all. Don't you think I'd like to be in your position and be able to do all those things? Do you think I like being a dummy and from the wrong side of the tracks and getting left out?"

"Oh, Highpockets," she said, "I didn't know you felt so left out." She took a hesitant step in his direction. "That's awful. I'm so sorry."

"Forget it," he said gruffly. "It doesn't matter. I just said it to try to get you to see what you're missing. Come on. Let's go. I'm freezing."

Leo started walking along the path that led to the main road. Pookie followed behind him in the still shadows that dipped around them in their slow thoughtful pace.

Leo slept soundly once he got himself to stop shivering. He woke up with the clear morning light when he heard Mr. Baines clumping down the hallway. Instead of jumping out of bed the way he sometimes did, he stared at the ceiling and thought about his swimming venture.

He really didn't know if he had saved Pookie or if she had saved him. He doubted if they would ever know. Maybe she would have sunk in the cold water, with or without him; or maybe some inner strength would have pulled her back. What mattered was that she had tried to help him when he needed it most.

It looked as if it were going to be another beautiful day. He sat up and pulled the summer-weight blanket around his neck. Suddenly the terror he had felt as he was drowning overwhelmed him. He remembered every detail with clarity and began to tremble. It made him feel sick to his stomach.

"Leo! You awake? Ethel's got the bacon sizzling just for you." Mr. Baines rapped on the door and then shuffled back to his own room, clumping and banging as he did every morning.

The last thing Leo wanted at that moment was bacon. Just the thought of it was pretty sickening. Getting up the courage to go to Mink, and then almost drowning, had about drained his stamina and appetite. What would his mother think if she heard about it?

He slowly swung his legs to the side of the bed and let them hang over. She probably would have told him that what he did was right. If his daddy were alive, he would have said the same thing. And George sure would have agreed. "Nothing ventured, nothing gained" was one of George's mottoes.

Leo slowly stood up and began dressing.

Life was full of risks. Every time you crossed the street, you took your life in your hands. There were just some things you had to go ahead and do, no matter what might happen. And the only way to learn how to swim was to practice it.

But not alone. That was where he had made his big mistake. As it turned out, he had Pookie there to help him, but he hadn't gone in the water with that assurance. No, there was no question about it. His mother would have agreed. He had made an error in judgment, but that could be corrected.

Leo and Mr. Baines spent the next few days fishing, inspecting lean-to sites, day-dreaming on the porch with their iced tea and Cokes, and organizing their fishing tackle. Leo figured it was about the one-thousandth time they had taken out the trout flies, held them up to the light, and put them back in their cases. He never knew quite what they were looking for, but he squinted and frowned and nodded just the way he knew he was supposed to.

He had seen very little of Pookie. She usually appeared just before lunch with Tigger, but only briefly before they went off, presumably swimming. At lunchtime she was silent as always and ate like a bird. Then she disappeared for the afternoons and only showed herself in time for dinner. And after dinner she was gone again.

Leo's appetite was back to normal, and he concentrated on his food at mealtimes so he wouldn't have to think anymore about Pookie and Tigger. The summer was almost over. It was too short, as always. His dumb school didn't get out until late June, and then he had to be back in classes right after Labor Day. That really only gave him a little over two months' vacation.

The rich kids who went to prep school got almost twice that. Tigger had told him they were out the end of May and didn't go back until way into September. Boy, that would be all right.

Leo's stomach began to rumble. He sucked in his breath and shifted his eyes sideways to see if Mr. Baines was looking at him.. The old man was fingering a bright yellow bass popper and making little smacking sounds with his lips. It was another hour until lunchtime. Leo hoped he could last. He'd had two eggs and four pieces of toast for breakfast, with lots of homemade raspberry jam made from berries Ethel herself had picked. He'd also had orange juice and a big glass of milk.

His stomach rumbled again. He shifted forward in his chair. "Want some iced tea, Mr. Baines?"

"That might taste pretty good. Make it weak so I can have two or so."

"Yes, sir." Leo stood up, but before he could take a step, the screen door opened and Tigger stepped out.

"Tigger, my boy!" Mr. Baines smiled. "You're up pretty early. Or is my watch wrong?" He hiked up his shirt-sleeve and looked at the gold watch on his twisted and swollen wrist.

"No," Tigger answered. "It's only eleven. Pookie's up, and I thought we might as well go on down to the lake for a bit."

"Good idea. Where is Pookie?"

"She'll be here in a minute." Tigger went to the railing and looked out across the meadow toward the mountains. "Nice and clear today."

Miss Maudie came out of the screen door, followed by the barking dogs, who scrambled over each other to reach the railing and look out between the top and bottom rails. They all were barking furiously.

"Stop that! Stop that, I say!" Miss Maudie yelled at them. "No! Darn fools saw a deer from the upstairs porch and about drove themselves wild to get down here and scream at it. No! Stop that!"

"Is this the first deer they've seen?" Mr. Baines asked innocently, looking at Leo and winking.

"I'm not going to answer a fool question like that. They just got excited about this one. I have no idea why. Stop that!" Miss Maudie clapped her hands together.

The dogs quieted down and began milling around the porch.

Mr. Baines went on, "They see approximately ten or more deer a day, for three and a half months in the summer, and have been seeing them for some years. If they meet one on the road, they tend to tuck their tails between their legs and run for home. Yet when they see one from the upstairs porch, they think it's a brand-new alien arrival just landed on the planet. Bright dogs."

Tigger turned and smiled at his grandfather. "So what else is new, Grandpa?"

"You two can go right ahead and make fun of them, and it won't matter a bit to any one of them. They rise above this sort of remark." Miss Maudie plopped down in a slatted armchair and clucked her tongue at the dogs. Tossie came at once and licked her hand. Nectarine and Louisa had to chew on each other a bit, but they finally tumbled toward her with their tails wagging.

"Rain on the way," Miss Maudie said.

Leo looked at the clear sky with its deep blue color above them paling near the distant mountains. There wasn't a cloud to be seen. Mr. Baines and Tigger made no comment, as if this was just the pronouncement they expected from her. But Leo was less sure. "Rain?" he asked.

"Yes," she answered. "By late afternoon there will be little puffy clouds across the sky, and during the night it will begin to rain. This sky is what's known as a weather breeder. At least, it is here in the mountains."

"Know how long the rain will last, Miss Maudie?" Tigger asked.

"Oh, not long," she said. "This isn't a real change, the kind that comes in from the west. This is just a little rain." She looked around. "You're up early. Any sign of Pookie?"

"She'll be here in a minute. We're going swimming. Probably just as well we're planning a longer time today, if it'll be raining tomorrow."

"Yes," Miss Maudie said.

Leo was still standing there, not having advanced very far. "Anyone else want iced tea? Miss Maudie?"

"No, thank you, Leo. While you're in there, get yourself a cooky to hold you until lunch."

Leo turned toward the screen door. Boy, she was a mind reader. Or maybe his stomach had been growling the whole time she'd been out here, and he just hadn't noticed. He put his hand on the door handle, but it opened before he could pull.

Pookie stepped out dressed in a little skimpy green one-piece bathing suit, with a big towel hanging from her hand.

Leo's mouth dropped open, and he stepped back from the door.

"Hi," Pookie said softly, smiling at him.

"Oh, there are you are, Pookie, darling," Mr. Baines said. "Going for a dip?"

"It appears Pookie has on her serious-swimming outfit," Miss Maudie said, staring Pookie right in the eye.

Pookie bent her head. "Yes," she said, "I need the exercise."

150

"Good," Miss Maudie said and looked back out across the meadow, a little smile on her lips.

Leo couldn't get over it. He had never seen Pookie in anything but long underwear and big men's shirts. She wasn't very big around, but she looked good in that suit. It was the color green that probably made her look like a mermaid underwater.

"Grandpa," Pookie began, "think you could spare Leo? He might like to swim with us."

Mr. Baines turned a startled look on Leo. "Why, certainly. If he wants to go."

Leo protested, "No, that's all right. I was about to get something for Mr. Baines." He could feel his neck turning hot and red.

"Nonsense," Mr. Baines said. "I can get my own iced tea. You go right ahead, Leo."

"No, that's all right . . ."

"Come on," Pookie said. "Tigger knows how you can swim, and he wants you to come, too."

Leo looked at Tigger.

Tigger turned his head and said casual-like, "Might as well come. It'll rain tomorrow, and you won't be able to swim then. And practice does make perfect."

Pookie tipped her head toward him and smiled. "Come on," she said very quietly.

Leo knew he was about to make an absolute idiot of himself, but he figured what the heck. "Okay." He looked at the floor. "I'll get my trunks." And then he really blushed. Tigger and all that crowd just swam in their cut-off blue jeans, but here he had these real proper trunks, like jerks and dummies wore. Well, that's all he had and there it was. "I'll be right down." He raced into the house and toward his bedroom, his heart and his head both swelling with excitement.

Tigger dived off the end of the big dock and surfaced halfway to the raft, which appeared to be *way* out, though Leo supposed it was about the same fifty feet it usually was. He wondered if he'd ever be good enough to get that far. Once Tigger neared the raft, he veered to the side of it and headed out for Sunfish Rock.

Leo looked at Sunfish Rock and tried to imagine it in deep shadow, with only some moonlight spread on its surface. He closed his eyes to thin slits and stared through his feathery lashes to get an image. It didn't look ghostly at all, drenched in sunlight the way it was now.

He looked down at his white legs sticking out from the wide-legged tan trunks. He felt like such a fool, but Tigger and Pookie appeared not to have noticed.

Leo couldn't get over Pookie's appearance. The bathing suit was strange enough, but her eyes seemed all sparkly and clear. He'd never seen them like that. When he had missed seeing her the past few days, she hadn't been holed up someplace stoned the way he'd thought, but must have been sleeping, resting, exercising, eating, and doing all the things normal people do. Or she had been having a bad time of it, trying not to get stoned, and doing a bang-up job of pulling out of it. Any way you looked at it, she had come out all right.

Pookie climbed down the ladder at the end of the dock, just as if she didn't know how to dive, and gracefully swam to the raft and back with no effort. Mr. Baines was right: she swam like a seal.

Once Leo was in the water, she gave him helpful hints and encouraged him. They went back and forth together at a slow pace, never getting too far from the dock and safety.

Leo was thankful Tigger didn't hang around while he was practicing. He seemed to be in the water for a serious purpose, judging by the number of times he went back and forth between the raft and the rock.

Finally Pookie climbed out of the water and stretched out on her towel on the dock. "Keep it up," she called to him, waving her hand and smiling.

Leo made four more back-and-forth laps, then climbed out and sat beside Pookie. "I think I've got the hang of it. I'll just try to practice when no one's around."

"Who will mind if you practice? We all had to start out just the way you're doing. You're just a little later, that's all. You don't have to be a champion to swim around here."

Leo lifted his chin and stared across the lake. She

was right. No one would make fun of him here. In town, people would hoot and holler at anyone who made a dumb move. Well, except his mother, of course. She wouldn't ever embarrass anyone.

One time the town drunk, old Maybelle Allen, had fallen into a big mud puddle in the parking lot of the hotel, and struggle as she might, she couldn't get her feet in the right place to get up; so she just sat back and unscrewed a bottle of gin and tipped her head back and drank it. Of course, everyone in sight had shrieked and shouted and slapped their thighs, doubling over with laughter. But when his mother marched out of the hotel and stepped right in the mud and took the town drunk's arm, saying, "Let me give you a hand, Maybelle, honey. This spring mud is awful on your clothes," then everybody shut up and looked the other way, pretending not to have seen anything. Two of the men even rushed over to help.

Pookie rolled onto her stomach. "Tigger says he met your mother out at the hotel."

Leo's heart stopped beating. He felt his face go red, and he turned his head away from Pookie. Tears sprang to his eyes, and he bit his lip real hard to get the tears under control.

"He told her you were a big help to Grandpa and how much everyone liked you." Pookie rolled back and sat up. "And she's going to have a baby. That'll be nice for you, to have someone little to watch growing up. Bet you'll have to do a bit of baby-sitting."

A great ringing went off in Leo's head. He had hoped never to have to admit to anyone in here that his mother was pregnant. He struggled to find his voice. "Yeah, I guess," he said, swallowing hard.

"Our mother has a little boy. He's two. I should say, we have a brother who's two. I don't think about him too much, though, as we never see him." She fiddled with a sliver of wood she pulled from the dock, jabbing it between the boards and scraping it along the crack. Finally she said, "I told you they live in Mexico."

"How come Tigger was at the hotel?"

"Oh, I don't know. He goes out sometimes at night, and I guess he stops in to have a beer." She let the sliver fall through to the water. "Does your daddy work at the hotel, too?"

"My daddy's dead."

"Oh, sorry. I really am. You probably told me and I forgot. Then you've got a stepfather?"

Leo really didn't want to get mad at her. If he told her it was none of her business, he was afraid she'd crumple like a house of cards. She wasn't one to stand up to severe criticism. Actually, he doubted she'd ever had any. If she got put down by George the way he, Leo, did, she would probably drown herself in an excess of hurt and bewilderment. It was a good thing he was tough, with a lot of moral fortitude, as George said he had: "I can fix anything from the crack of dawn to a broken heart except a lack of moral fortitude. If you don't have that, you're just out of luck in my book. Leo here's got a good share of it." George said that the time Leo admitted he was the one who had broken the refrigerator door when he could easily have pretended it was someone else.

"I might have a stepfather someday, but I don't now," he admitted. "My mother lives with George, but they're not married yet." His mother once said they'd get married in time, but she wasn't yet ready to take on a new name and a new commitment. That was before she was pregnant. Leo expected she'd be ready once the baby was born.

"Oh," Pookie said quietly.

The sun was warm on Leo's shoulders, but he felt himself shivering. He wished he had never come down here today. If he had stayed back and eaten cookies and put a stick in Mr. Baines's iced tea, he wouldn't be in this pickle now.

"We have a lot in common," Pookie finally said. "Our mother's not married either. The big difference is that she says she's never going to get married. Something to do with inheritance in a foreign country, where a husband might have some kind of claim on her money. Manuel, the man she lives with, is dying to marry her. But she just says no." Pookie now traced her finger around the water stain on the bare boards of the dock. "It's real hard on Grandpa. But he and Miss Maudie are just an older generation and don't take changes in moral codes too well. Of course, he's thrilled whenever Mother comes for a visit, but that's not very often. I think she knows he's unhappy about her living in sin."

Leo stared at Pookie with an open mouth. He could hardly believe his ears. "Do you mind?"

"Mind? If she's not married? Oh, no. I did at first, but not anymore. The only thing I mind is that she doesn't come see us very much."

"And Tigger? How does he feel?"

"The same as I do."

"Why don't you go see her?" Leo asked.

"We tried, but it's not a happy situation. We were too much like outsiders. We felt like sore thumbs, standing out and nobody wanting us. So we don't go anymore."

"But sometimes she comes to see you."

"Once or twice a year. And then she leaves Manuel in Mexico. She leaves the baby there, too, with a nurse."

Leo couldn't get over it. Leaving Pookie and Tigger was much worse than what his mother did. "But she must love you." Though maybe not as much as his mother loved him.

"Sure," Pookie said, "I think she probably does. Come on, I'll race you to the raft."

Without thinking, Leo scrambled to his feet and followed Pookie into the water with a big splash.

Miss Maudie had sure been right about the weather. The clear blue sky began to fill up with little puffy white clouds by mid-afternoon, and when Leo went to bed that night, it had already begun to rain.

He had stayed awake a long time listening to the rain spatter against the house, a distant rhythm that echoed and re-echoed as his mind got more and more tangled up with thoughts.

He felt he was on a seesaw after talking to Pookie. It seemed that their mothers had a lot in common. Neither of their reasons for not getting married had much to do with all that love stuff people were always talking about.

And babies. Pookie's mother had gone ahead and had a baby without being married, just as his mother was going to do. Rich people were just like poor people when it came to some things, or even a lot of things.

Leo didn't know what to think anymore. He had been so mad at his mother and George. But if Pookie and Tigger could accept what their mother had done, why couldn't he? Pookie wasn't embarrassed when she talked about her mother. She was just sad that she didn't see much of her. She was sad for herself and for Tigger.

Leo drifted in and out of sleep all night. It would soon be time to get up. Any minute now he would hear Mr. Baines coughing and hacking in his room; then the slow, hesitant clump to the bathroom would follow. He would knock on Leo's door on his return trip and then bang around in his bedroom, getting dressed and buckling the brace on. He didn't want anyone to help him in the mornings. He was as independent as could be. By nighttime, it was a different matter.

This was the day of the club meeting. Usually only members and their families went to the meetings, but Mr. Baines had gotten special permission to include Leo. Leo knew this was an honor. He had never seen all the members in one spot. He supposed that Pookie wouldn't bother to go, but Tigger probably figured he had to. He had to represent the next generation about to take over the management of the club.

The snoring choked to an abrupt halt, and the coughing began. The day was beginning. In spite of his troubled thoughts, Leo was hungry. He could sure go for a mess of Ethel's pancakes with the melting butter on top and plenty of hot syrup in a pitcher. Maybe a few sausage patties on the side.

He jumped up and began to dress, not waiting for Mr. Baines to knock. This was a day he had been looking forward to most of the summer. He could hardly wait to hear Mr. Baines give his lean-to report. He felt proud that he had been a part of the old man's committee. They had never gotten around to asking Peggy Maitland to join them, and while Miss Maudie was officially the other member, she had left it all to her brother and Leo.

Leo opened his door just as Mr. Baines was about to knock.

"Well, Leo, looks like you beat me to it. All that swimming yesterday must have made you sleep pretty soundly and wake yourself up raring to go."

"Yes, sir, I guess it did."

"Good. Too bad it's raining today. But tomorrow you can get in some more swimming with Pookie and Tigger. Don't know why I didn't get you down there before now."

"That's all right. We've been pretty busy doing other things."

"Yes, I guess we have at that. Well, we can give a good report when Creeper calls on us."

"Yes, sir."

"Of course, he hasn't announced officially that

we've been appointed. I guess other members don't know what we've been up to. Well, that's all right. The greatest pleasure comes from doing something only you know you've done. Secret rewards. There's nothing like them. You and I know, and that's the main thing, isn't it?"

"Yes, sir. We've done a good job."

"You wait downstairs, and I'll be with you in a minute. I might even have some of Ethel's pancakes myself this morning. I'm feeling pretty good. Pretty good."

Leo smiled. He was feeling pretty good, too.

Leo could sure see why Pookie had stayed at home. The meeting was long and slow, and he was getting pretty restless sitting on the hard wooden chair. Sheets of paper were distributed with columns of figures, and they went over every penny that had been spent in the past year. Someone would ask a question about why the charges for firewood had gone up, and the treasurer would explain that. Fifteen minutes later, someone else would look up from the fact sheets and ask the same question. There would be a lot of sighing and groaning, and the treasurer or Creeper McGraw would go over the whole thing again.

Leo squirmed and stared out the window at the rain and wished they would hurry and get to the committee reports. He looked around the big room with its dark paneling and mounted deer heads. Over the huge stone fireplace was a stuffed brook trout caught by Mrs. Babcock in 1955, all recorded on a brass plaque underneath the fish. Boy, it sure would make Mr. Baines happy if he caught a fish like that. He could hear it now, the old man churning along in the Jeep, going from cottage to cottage to tell how the fish jumped, dived, ran out all the line, and damn near broke the rod.

Leo's daydreaming came to a halt when he heard the word "committee." He sat up straight and looked sideways at Mr. Baines, who was hunched down in his chair with his neck sticking out, peering over his glasses at Creeper McGraw with an absolutely blank face. He could have been any one of the people in the room who had never heard of the lean-to committee. But not Leo: he tensed as his heartbeat picked up speed.

They heard from the trail committee, the fish committee, the hunting committee, the house committee, and the club historian. Then Creeper McGraw shuffled his papers around and got everyone's attention.

"There has been a suggestion we have a new committee to supervise the picnic areas and lean-tos. There have been some unfortunate incidents of people not picking up their trash when they leave, and while these have been few, we hope they won't happen again. This new committee would oversee all that, as well as the firewood and the condition of the balsam needles in the lean-tos. Those of us who like to sleep in the lean-tos consider this last responsibility to be of utmost importance."

Everyone laughed and made little comments.

The president continued, "Rastus seems to have been on top of this all summer, but he has a lot to do without having to go around checking the picnic sites. If everyone is in agreement about this new committee"—and here he looked around the room to make sure no one objected—"then we can proceed with it. I'll appoint a chairman, and the chairman can get two or three members to assist." He paused. "It seems to me the ideal person for this would be Peggy Maitland. I've asked her if she would undertake it, and she has agreed. Now, is there any unfinished business?"

A terrible ringing was going off in Leo's ears. He looked at Mr. Baines, who was motionless, waiting for the meeting to come to an end. It couldn't be true. It just couldn't. Creeper McGraw himself was the one who had asked Mr. Baines to head the lean-to committee way back in the beginning of the summer. He couldn't have forgotten. But he had. Leo wanted to jump up and shout at him, but of course he just sat there staring at the beaked nose jutting out from the steel-rimmed glasses and the sharp bony chin sunk downward.

Leo slowly turned his head and looked around the

room. Miss Maudie was still sitting straight and stiff in her chair, looking at the president. Other people were putting away their reading glasses and standing up. It was all over. He saw Peggy Maitland smiling and chatting cheerfully, just as if she had been in charge of lean-tos all along. Leo hated her. He hated Creeper McGraw.

Mr. Baines stood up, slowly, leaning heavily on the arm of the chair. He had to step on his bad leg several times before he could get it to support his weight. He reached over and gripped Leo's shoulder, leaning on it as he took a weighty step toward the door. Then he released Leo and lurched forward.

Leo jumped up and walked behind him, not looking to the right or left, not wanting to see the smiling faces. Outside the big meeting room Mr. Baines struggled to get his arms into his raincoat, which had been hanging on a wall peg near the front door. Leo held the coat, and between them they got the coat onto Mr. Baines's stooped figure.

Once in the Jeep, with Mr. Baines slumped in the passenger seat and Leo behind the wheel, a gray gloom settled over them. The rain beat on the canvas top of the Jeep. The stale air inside was depressingly close; the lingering smell of dead fish and wet boots became almost suffocating.

Leo rolled down his window a little and started the engine. He eased the Jeep into gear and headed up the road, not looking at those walkers who stepped aside and waved them by with a friendly gesture. They were false. They were all false.

"I don't understand," Leo said. "Mr. McGraw promised that to you. How could he have done that? He's a downright liar and a cheat."

"You watch your tongue!" Mr. Baines turned on him fiercely. "You young whippersnapper, don't you dare call Creeper McGraw a liar! He's a fine person and an excellent president! You mind yourself and never criticize him or anyone else in here!"

Stunned by the outburst, Leo cringed behind the wheel. He could feel tears spring to his eyes. He drew his lips into a thin line and bit hard on them. He stared at the road and steered the Jeep around the corner and down to the big house.

Leo stepped out into the rain and went to the other side of the Jeep, opening the door for Mr. Baines. But he didn't offer to help him get out, the way he usually did. He stood back and watched as the old man struggled to get his heavy braced leg out and then himself into an upright position. He looked away, up the rain-drenched road, until the old man was away from the Jeep; then he shut the door.

Instead of following Mr. Baines into the house, Leo went the other direction, toward the long porch that bordered the meadow. He went up the steps and sat in one of the Adirondack chairs. He couldn't remember when he had felt so terrible. He had done the unforgivable and gotten the old man mad at him. He had dared to criticize, something he now knew he should never have done, even though the criticism was deserved.

He felt like a black hole quietly folding in on itself. He wished he were young enough to cry. He had lost so much, in so little time. Nothingness. That's what he felt like. Nothingness. In oblivion. One time George had said, "Leo could amount to something if he doesn't just hunker down to oblivion." Leo hadn't known what oblivion meant at the time and had looked it up. Now he really knew. Nothingness. And that's just where he felt he was now—in some big void. Everyone had lied to him. He had been betrayed. He had thought he was important to the old man, but he wasn't. He was nothing but a young whippersnapper needed to fetch and carry and row the boat, and that was all.

Leo was so sunk in his misery that he didn't hear anyone come out onto the porch, but when he raised his head Miss Maudie was sitting in the chair next to his.

"Oh," he said, startled, and sat forward. "I didn't know you were there."

Miss Maudie just pressed her thin lips together and stared ahead.

Leo figured he must be in her bad book now, too.

Mr. Baines had undoubtedly said something mean about him as soon as he saw his sister. He didn't know what to say to her, so he just waited.

Presently Miss Maudie spoke up, "That Creeper McGraw makes me so darned mad. Wouldn't surprise me one bit if he had gotten to the top of the corporate ladder by cheating. What did he think he was doing by passing over Grandpa? I don't suppose it was deliberate. I just think he forgot—forgot all about Grandpa, as if he didn't exist. It makes me mad. There's no excuse for it."

Leo had never heard her refer to Mr. Baines as "Grandpa" to him before. She always said "My brother" or "Mr. Baines" very formally when she was talking to Leo.

Miss Maudie tapped her skinny fingers on the arm of the chair. The blue veins stood out on her hands, and brown spots dotted the skin. They were the hands of the old. Leo had seen them plenty, out in town, but there the blue veins and brown spots also had rough red skin. His mother used lots of hand lotion. She said, "The harsh elements and peeling potatoes in icy water are awful hard on your skin." His mother took care of herself, so she would stay young-looking and pretty. It was a good thing she did. Leo liked her to look pretty.

"Grandpa about took my head off when I came in. You'd better watch out, or he'll be snappy with you next," Miss Maudie said.

"He's already done it," Leo answered.

"Already? Then I'm the second one. I had thought I was the first. I told Pookie to get to her room and stay there until the storm passed. She's overly sensitive and gets upset when he snaps at her. Tigger just lets it ride over him like a wave." She worked her lips in little twitches. "Well, don't get downcast about it. He doesn't mean any harm. He just lashes out at everything in his path when he gets hurt and angry. Always has, even when he was a tiny boy." She smiled. "I've been around it for so long, I guess I'm used to it." She looked at Leo. "But you aren't, are you?"

"No, ma'am."

She looked back across the meadow. "He won't even remember he was snappy with you when he calms down. Try not to take offense."

"No, ma'am."

"I know it's hard. But think of Grandpa. He's been hurt, and his dignity's been stripped away from him. He's been made to feel old and useless."

"But he's not!"

"I know that. But that's the way he feels. And on top of that, this weather is bad on his arthritis. Whenever it rains, he's in a lot of pain. As a matter of fact, he's in pain most of the time and tries to hide it. That little toddy in his iced tea helps ease the aching."

"You know about that?"

She smiled. "Who do you think keeps the bottle full in the pantry?"

Leo's mouth dropped open. Well, what do you know. All this time he thought he and the old man were putting one over on Miss Maudie. "I guess I thought he did it."

"No, I'm the one. It's probably not good for him, but it can't hurt too much. He's lost a lot in his lifetime. A little pick-me-up seems a harmless thing as compensation. You just be patient with him. You and he have had a good summer, and there's no point in letting it get ruined now. It's a silly business, but there it is. You and I will get over being snapped at. He's old and he might not get over being forgotten and passed over." She stood up. "That boring meeting went on for so long, I don't have time to do much with lunch. Maybe we'll just have grilled ham-and-cheese sandwiches. That sound all right to you?"

"Yes, ma'am. It sure does. You want me to help you?"

"No, you just be here for Grandpa when he comes out. He might need an extra drop in his iced tea today. And just shut your ears if he's still storming around."

Leo watched Miss Maudie go into the house. Sometimes she reminded him of his mother. Mr. Baines said, "You have to get up pretty early in the morning to fool Miss Maudie." George said, "Your mother never misses a trick." That made them a lot alike in Leo's book.

B y mid-afternoon the rains had stopped. Mr. Baines hobbled into the kitchen where Leo and Pookie sat making plans. He paused by the table and let his hand fall on Leo's shoulder.

"Just what are you two cooking up?" he asked.

"A hike down to Mink," Pookie answered, smiling at him. "But we can go fishing if you'd rather."

"No, darling, I think it's time Leo got out with someone his own age. Being stuck with an old man all summer isn't always much fun, though we've had our share of good times. Isn't that right?" He patted Leo's shoulder.

Leo wanted to reach up and take the old man's hand, but he knew he couldn't do that. "It sure is right," he said lamely.

"And I guess you've learned to take the good with the bad—might even say you've had a lion's share of the latter."

"It's been good," Leo said quickly. "The whole summer's been good." He looked across the table at Pookie, who had her eyes on the old man.

"Everyone has a bad day, Grandpa," she said smiling at him. "I've had plenty."

"If you have, no one remembers them, Pookie, darling."

She ducked her head and looked into her lap, her teeth pressing into her bottom lip.

Leo felt a tremor run through the bony hand and into his shoulder. He didn't know what to say.

"Tell you what," Mr. Baines said, breaking the awkward silence. "You two run on down there and have a swim, and I'll come along in an hour or so and pick you up."

"You don't want to drive that bucking Jeep," Leo said, turning his head to Mr. Baines. "I think it's stiffened up lately; it about wrenches my arms out of the sockets to turn the wheel."

"It always has been hell on me. That's why I like to have you drive it. But it won't hurt me this one time."

Leo looked at Pookie. "No, sir, I guess it won't."

"The exercise both ways would be good for me, Grandpa," Pookie said. "I'm still not as strong as I should be."

"You would deprive me of the pleasure of seeing you and Leo swim. I hear you're pretty good, Leo. Pretty good. One seal and one lion." He chuckled.

"That's a sight I'd like to see." He turned away from Leo, dragging one leg. "Why don't we see what kind of cookies Ethel made for us today? I'll have one first, then fix myself a little iced tea. Never did think sweet cookies went with tea, hot or cold."

Leo and Pookie walked down to Mink Pond through the deep woods that paralleled the road, taking a trail neither of them had been on all summer. The woods smelled of damp leaves and wet earth, rich, heady smells that mingled with the sounds of still-dripping trees.

After they had been in the lake for a good thirty minutes and Pookie had given Leo some advanced instructions, they split up. Leo stayed near the dock and practiced. Pookie streaked out toward the middle, the water rippling past her as she swam expertly and easily away.

Leo knew he had improved a lot in just two lessons. He wasn't afraid anymore. He didn't care if anyone came along and saw him. In fact, he rather hoped they would. He looked pretty good. Pretty good.

By the time they both climbed out of the water, Leo's body had a healthy pink glow. He rubbed his face and head with the towel and squeezed the water out of the clinging legs of his trunks.

Pookie sat down on the dock with the towel around her thin shoulders. "The air's cold after all that rain."

She bent forward with her knees pulled up and put her fingertips to her lips.

"The sun feels good," Leo said, though he also felt cold.

"It's not as warm as it was a month ago. Fall is coming. We've all got to go back to school."

"I know. I'm not much looking forward to that."

"Neither am I. Tigger is anxious to get back. He wants to get his boat together and start practicing. You know, his boat for crew. He loves it so much. He loves racing other boats."

Leo had never seen crew races, so he couldn't quite picture this. "Do you have to have a lot of money to race?" he asked. "The boats must be expensive."

"Oh, they are. But the university buys those. No, you don't have to have money. No more than you do to play football. It's one of the school sports."

Leo bet you did have to have money. It sounded pretty exclusive. "All you people are so rich," he suddenly said. "There are so many things you take for granted without thinking about how much they cost. It must be nice to be rich."

"We aren't all rich," Pookie said with surprise in her voice. "Don't think that for a minute. Oh, our mother has plenty of money, and Tigger and I go to expensive schools and all that. But we don't have much spending money of our own. Miss Maudie has a lot of money because she's a good manager and a shrewd investor.

Grandpa doesn't have any money at all."

Leo stared at her. "What did you say?"

"I said Grandpa doesn't have any money at all. He long ago spent all his. Bad investments. He had to sell his apartment and everything. He lives with Miss Maudie. She set up a trust for him so he would have some income, not much, but enough to go out for lunch and dinner and things like that. But she controls the money."

"Mr. Baines doesn't have *any* money?"

"No, not a penny of his own." She smiled. "He doesn't care. He's perfectly happy living the way he does. Of course, it's a good thing Miss Maudie didn't lose hers. I don't know where we'd be if she had. Maybe we'd all be living in Mexico and hating it." She lifted her head and looked behind her. "I hear Grandpa coming. Wait till he sees what a good swimmer you are."

After dinner, Mr. Baines wanted to go over the fishing tackle again. "The water's nice and cool after all that rain. The bass ought to be biting tomorrow morning."

The old man seemed cheerful, but Leo doubted that he'd forgotten Creeper McGraw's slight. It still nagged at Leo, but then his mind was so full of surprises and mixed emotions he could hardly think straight at all. This had sure been a day of revelations.

So they lined up the frogs and other hair bugs, the poppers, the tiny silver lures with a single hook, and even a few trout streamers just in case they couldn't entice a bass and had to go for trout instead. They pored over them far into the night, even after Pookie had gone to bed. Tigger was at Beek's (or so he had said), and Miss Maudie was out somewhere, probably playing bridge with her cronies. Leo really wanted to go to bed, too, but he didn't dare say so. Mr. Baines didn't seem tired at all. Leo wondered if the old man was avoiding going upstairs to his bedroom where he would be alone with his misery. If only he could tell him, "Never mind. What does it matter if that jerk Creeper McGraw forgot about you? You're you, and that's what matters." That's the sort of thing his mother would say. George, too.

So they checked over their equipment, pulling the line off the reel and walking as far as they could with it, from the end of the living room to the far corner of the back hallway, then rewinding it; staring down the length of the rod to make sure it was still straight and the guides were lined up; wiping off the reel; and generally doing all the things that were unnecessary to do as they had been done umpteen times in the recent past.

"Listen," Mr. Baines suddenly said, "I hear them coming."

Leo listened. Sure enough, there was the sound of a

truck. But he had no idea who it was this time of night.

The dogs, who had been quietly sleeping on the sofa, suddenly jumped up and ran into the back hall, whining and barking. They only acted like this when Miss Maudie was coming back. Someone must have given her a ride home.

Sure enough, the back door soon opened, and Leo could hear Miss Maudie's voice in the back hallway.

"Down! There you are! Stop that barking! Quiet! Good girl."

And then there was the sound of a man's voice.

"Come on in!" Mr. Baines shouted. "We're still up."

Miss Maudie came into the room, followed by the leaping dogs and the towering figure of Erastus Pike, his crumpled gray hat squarely on his head. Miss Maudie held a spinning rod in one hand and a flashlight in the other. Even across the room, Leo could see the sparkling and hear the jangling of the bright metal hooks secured to the rod.

"Look what we got! Show 'em, Rastus," Miss Maudie said triumphantly.

Rastus grinned and held up a long-handled bass net sagging with the weight of fish. "Yup," he said. "Two twenty-one-inch large-mouths and three more darned near that big."

Twenty-one-inch large-mouth bass! And caught at night, with multihooked lures and a flashlight! Leo almost fell over backward.

176

"Well, I'll be," Mr. Baines murmured.

"Stubborn old goat," Miss Maudie said to him, smiling. "You ought to come out with us some night and have some fun. See these, Leo? You won't catch anything like this rowing around the lake in the daytime with some fancy fly-fishing equipment."

"Don't listen to her, Leo," Mr. Baines said. "She's never understood the finer points of fishing."

"I understand one thing," she said, propping her spinning rod in a corner. "Seeing's believing, and you can see for yourself what we've got here." She pulled her arms out of her jacket and hung it across the back of a chair. "One of these fish will feed all of us for lunch tomorrow. How about a drink to warm you up, Rastus?"

"No, thank you, Maudie. I'd best be getting on up to the house."

"I've got some root beer," she said.

"Next time. We've had a fine night of it. Maybe next week we can have another go."

"Good. Now just leave us one of those fish, and you take the rest." She pointed at the sparkling collection of hooks on the spinning rod. "With a good outfit like that, we can get us some fish whenever we want. Go on, now, and take those fish."

Leo swallowed and looked past Mr. Baines to Miss Maudie and Rastus. "That's the kind of fishing my mother likes to do," he said in a clear voice.

"She's right," Miss Maudie said.

Leo thought he saw Rastus's eyes narrow a tiny bit and a trace of a smile come across his lips.

"Then you'd better get her in here, Leo, so you and I can straighten her out," Mr. Baines said.

Miss Maudie laughed. "You've always been jealous of anyone doing something better than you can do it. You ought to just admit we catch a lot more fish and have a lot more fun; then you ought to join us."

"Catch more fish!" Mr. Baines looked over the metal rims of his glasses. "That'll be the day. And I guess we know what fun is, don't we, Leo?"

"Yes, sir. But I guess they both sound like fun."

"You're a born diplomat, Leo," Miss Maudie said.

"Boy's right," Rastus said. "They're both fun." He looked Leo right in the eye.

Later, in bed, Leo thought about his mother and realized how much he had missed her over the summer. He was no longer ashamed of the way she looked—only of himself. He wondered if she had missed him. Of course, she had George to keep her from being lonely, and that sure must help a lot. He was glad George was there. It was no fun to be lonely.

And what would Pookie and the old people do next summer if Tigger got a job and wasn't with them? He knew how much they would miss Tigger.

Leo realized how lucky he was. He never had to be

alone, unless he just plain wanted to be. Why, if he really got blue being by himself, all he had to do was go to the hotel. Anybody in there would be glad to talk to him, seeing's how he was his mother's son and practically George's stepson.

Things were getting all mixed up in Leo's head: George and his mother, Mr. Baines who hadn't any money, so-called success stories like Creeper McGraw, and Pookie . . . Pookie with her mother way off in Mexico. Tigger could take care of himself, that much Leo knew. He wished Tigger hadn't gotten him to take the car keys from Mr. Baines's pocket; but that was Leo's fault, too. If Leo had refused, Tigger might have even had a lot of respect for him.

What did it matter if Mr. Baines had no money and Creeper McGraw was a double-crosser? He'd still had a good summer, hadn't he? People were what they were, and you just had to accept them on their own terms and not pretend to yourself or hope they were anything different. His mother was herself, and Leo now knew he would never want her to change. George might be a jerk, but one thing was for sure: he was just what he said he was. And he probably could fix anything from the crack of dawn to a broken heart.

It would all come clear to him. What the heck, he had plenty of time to learn.

The day came when Leo had to leave. He packed

his blue jeans and put on his baggy khakis, noticing that they weren't nearly as baggy as they had been two months before. He folded his shirts as best he could, which was none too good, but he didn't worry about that: his mother would straighten them out when he got home. He looked around his bedroom to make sure he hadn't forgotten anything.

Once downstairs, with his suitcase on the back side of the porch by the steps, he began to feel a queer mixture of sadness and anticipation. He was really sorry to go, and he hated the very idea of school; but he was anxious to be with his mother and George and his friends again.

He walked around to the far side of the porch, where Mr. Baines and Miss Maudie were sitting, looking across to the distant mountains and reminiscing.

"Remember the time we got lost trying to climb Cedar Mountain?" Mr. Baines asked.

"Only too well," Miss Maudie replied. "Mother was mad as a wet hen when she had to send the guide out to find us. Of course, we never should have gone without him."

"As I recall, he was busy guiding her and Father around some lake."

"No, he was drunk up in one of the waitresses' rooms, and that was what made her doubly mad."

"Oh, yes." Mr. Baines dipped his chin and chuckled. "I believe you're right. Yes, she was plenty mad.

Oh, there you are, Leo." He waved his twisted hand with the swollen joints in the air. "We were wondering where you were." He opened his tackle bag and pulled out a small box. "This is for you. It just might come in handy."

Leo took the box and opened it. Inside were six of Mr. Baines's favorite trout flies and three special bass poppers. Tears welled in his eyes. "Wow!" was all he could say.

"You never know when you'll have time to do a little fishing. There are always Saturdays."

"Only four before the season ends," Miss Maudie said.

"What season is that?" Mr. Baines asked, winking at Leo.

"The trout season," she snapped. "I assume that's what you're talking about."

"I just might be talking about the bass season, mightn't I?"

"I'm not going to pay any attention to you when you get like this. You just go ahead and babble away about whatever you want." Miss Maudie shifted in her chair and snapped her fingers together. Both Nectarine and Louisa jumped up and ran to her side. Tossie opened her eyes and wagged her tail, then went back to sleep.

"There you go again, stirring up the dogs. Why can't you just let them be when they're quiet?" Mr.

Baines chuckled again. "Incorrigible. That's what you are. Always have been."

Leo felt a swelling in his chest. He wished he could do something for the two old people. Suddenly he said, "Maybe you could come out to the hotel and see us someday. I'm there every afternoon after school. And my mother's there all the time."

"Why, wouldn't that be nice," Miss Maudie said. "We'll certainly try. Of course, we're only going to be here another week ourselves."

"Only another week?" Leo asked.

"Yes," Miss Maudie said. "Pookie and Tigger have to get ready to go back to school, not that that takes much preparation. Still, there are things to do."

"The truth of the matter is that it gets too cold about that time," Mr. Baines said. "I start to ache a bit. That insufferable heat in the apartment, unhealthy as it is, does make my bones feel better."

"Oh," Leo said, with a sinking feeling. He might never see them again.

"But there's always next summer," Mr. Baines said. "Maybe you'll be free to come in again. I'd say we'd had a pretty good summer. Pretty good."

"Yes, sir. Pretty good." He paused, then added: "But I may have to help out at the hotel next summer. My mother'll be tied up with the baby by then, and George might need me."

"Well, let's talk about that next summer, not now,"

Miss Maudie said. "No point in getting too far ahead of ourselves."

"I think I hear a car coming, Leo." Mr. Baines craned his neck around and peered toward the parking lot.

"It must be my mother. I'll ask her to come up and see you. I doubt she'll have time to go fishing today, but I know she'd like to say hello."

"Oh, splendid," Miss Maudie said.

"Grand," Mr. Baines said. "We can all have some iced tea."

Leo walked around the long side of the porch, slowing his steps to watch three tame deer that paused in their grazing to watch him. He thought back to his first day in here, looking over this same spot at some deer, probably the same ones. Pookie had come out all vague and whispery, hardly able to walk, and had been a total mystery to him.

He walked farther along the porch, realizing how much he was going to miss Pookie, and when he turned the corner toward the back of the house, he saw her, standing by his suitcase.

When he got near, she said, "Here's a car. Is that your mother?"

Leo looked at the clean, shining surface of George's car. "Yeah," he said, waving his hand at the driver. "That's my mother. Hi!" he called. His mother waved back and pulled up beside the Jeep.

Pookie smiled. "She looks nice. You're lucky."

"Yeah, I know," Leo answered. He couldn't think of anything else to say.

Pookie reached out and took his hand. "Will you come in next summer and swim with me?"

"I'd like that." He looked down at her small fingers holding his. "Maybe you can come out and see me in town."

"Oh, yes." She smiled. "Let's stay friends."

And Leo suddenly realized there was hope for him to become a lion. He had friends, he had people who loved him, and he felt good about himself. If he kept going that way, someday he could be king of his own world. And just offhand, he couldn't think of anything better than that. It was a pretty good world. Pretty good.